Killing Them Softly

An Erotic Tale of Murder

Roy Glenn

Escapism Entertainment
1038-5 Dunn Avenue
30
Jacksonville, FL 32218

ISBN-13: 9780982731611
ISBN-10: 0982731612

First Printing; November 2010

10 9 8 7 6 5 4 3 2 1

Also by Roy Glenn

Is It A Crime
Mob
Drug Related
Payback
Outlaw
In A Cold Sweat
No More Tears In The End
Three The Hard Way
Commit To Violence

Crime Of Passion
Body Of Evidence
Ulterior Motive

Girls From Da Hood
Around The Way Girls 4
Gigolos Get Lonely Too

Killing Them Softly

An Erotic Tale of Murder

Roy Glenn

Chapter One

Devin

I rolled over in bed and watched my wife Taye get up and go in the bathroom. No matter how many times it happened, or how I tried to condition myself to it, the result was always the same: the sex we had was uninspiring. But it hadn't always been like that.

In the three years that Taye and I have been married, we've gone through a lot. We met on the subway during rush hour. I would see her every morning getting on the train, and I watched and admired her for months, before I got up the courage to speak to her. To me, Taye was the most beautiful woman I had ever seen.

One Monday morning, I decided that I would talk to her, so I positioned myself in front of the door, reading the newspaper. When the door opened, the first thing Taye saw was me.

"Good morning," and a friendly smile, was all I offered up that first day, before I buried my head back in the paper.

Taye barely acknowledged my presence. She made eye contact, but quickly looked away without saying anything. Men always tried to talk to her on the train. I sat and watched her turn away man after man who tried to push up on her. To her, I was probably just another faceless and nameless man on the train.

On the second day, I posted up in the same spot, and when the door opened and Taye got on, I said, "Good morning." But this time I added, "How are you today?" And then I went right back to the paper. Once again, Taye didn't respond, but I could tell that this time she noticed me.

I stood there and feigned reading the paper, but Taye, as she did every day, had my undivided attention. I stood there, watching her reading her book—a novel called *Commit to Violence*. I checked out the look on her face as she read. It was like she was totally enthralled in whatever she was reading.

When Taye got on the train on the third day, I said, "Good morning. How are you?" Like I did the day before, but this time, I had to do a double take. "You look very nice today," I added at the sight of Taye in her black skirted suit.

"Thank you," Taye said, as she passed and moved to a spot to stand.

Instead of her usual ponytail, Taye let her hair hang down to her shoulders. We exchanged glances and smiles for the duration of the ride together that morning. And by the end of week, we had introduced ourselves.

Our relationship developed as a friendship at first; kind of an old-fashioned courtship. It was filled with long walks and picnic lunches in the park. We'd spend hours on the phone at night having long telephone conversations about everything, and nothing in particular. After a few weeks, we began meeting after work for drinks at first, and then dinner. Dinner turned into dinner and a movie. Dinner and a movie turned into dinner, a movie, and dancing.

"How did I get so lucky?" I asked her one night after we left the club.

"What do you mean?" Taye said, as we walked back to my car.

I stopped and turned to her. "How did I get so lucky to find you?"

"I guess you lived a good life." Taye smiled. "You're not like any other man I've met lately. You're a gentleman, and you took the time to get to know me. You made me feel like it was important to you; like I was important to you."

We stood there for a while; you know, having that moment. Looking into each other's eyes; feelin' that strong vibe. "No," I said, "that's not what I wanna ask you."

Taye took a step closer and smiled. Close enough to kiss. "Well, just what do you wanna ask me?"

It made me a little nervous to be so close to her. I held it together, but it wasn't easy. "Taye, you're an intelligent woman. You're funny, and you are so beautiful. How come you don't have a man?" My father told me once, when you meet a pretty woman and she doesn't have a man, find out why.

"Because he was a moron who didn't recognize much less appreciate what a good woman he had," Taye said.

"So do you think it would be all right if I kissed you?"

"I don't think I'd slap you, but we'll just have to see."

I took Taye into my arms and kissed her gently. She put her arms around my neck, and I allowed myself to get caught up in the moment.

That first kiss, the one I'd been thinking about since the first time I saw her, was everything that I imagined it would be. Taye kissed me like it had been a while since she'd kissed a man, and even longer since she'd kissed a man she actually liked. Taye told me later that during the last year of her relationship with the moron, any type of intimacy was more like an obligation than a pleasure shared, when two are in love. It was a task to be performed and nothing more.

That first kiss between us was tender and filled with passion. I really couldn't say how long we stood by the car kissing, but it was a long time.

When we finally separated from each other's arms, we both just kind of stood there in complete silence, staring at each other until Taye finally said, "Wow."

"Yeah," was all I could manage before unlocking her door.

As we drove to Taye's apartment, no words were spoken.

There were none needed. The sexual tension in that car was strong. We held hands and exchanged glances during the ride. Each time I had to stop for a red light, I would lean over and kiss Taye; allow my hands to roam over her body. Not wanting to seem overexcited by what I thought was about to happen, I really had to fight the urge to drive faster.

Once we got to Taye's apartment, she invited me in. "Can I get you something to drink?" Taye asked.

"Whatever you have is fine." And with that she disappeared.

I sat patiently on the couch until Taye reappear with a bottle of champagne in one hand and two glasses in the other. Taye filled my glass and handed it to me.

"Thank you," I said.

She smiled and poured herself glass. She raised the glass, and we both drained our glasses. Then I reached for her, touched her face and kissed her.

She picked up the bottle, took me by the hand, and led me into the bedroom. She turned on some light jazz and lit two candles, before sitting down next to me on the bed.

I looked at her and touched her face. "Taye, you are so beautiful."

I kissed her again and felt the warmth coming from her hands against my body. Taye pushed me down on the bed. I laid there on my back, enjoying the taste of her tongue darting playfully in and out of my month. The kissing continued, and we explored each other's bodies with our hands. Taye sat up and began to loosen my tie. "Let me help you with that," I offered.

"No," she whispered softly and moved my hands. Taye took off my tie, unbuttoned my shirt, and methodically ran her hands over my chest. The feeling made my whole body quiver.

Taye turned me the fuck on.

I watched as her tongue moved softly across my chest, lingering at m nipples. It sent chills through me.

Taye stood up and unzipped her dress, allowing it to fall to the floor before returning to the bed.

She lay next to me, dressed only in her bra and thong, and I enjoyed the warmth of her body against my skin. I ran my hands over every inch of her body. Now it was Taye's turn to quiver under my touch. I sat up and took off my shirt, without breaking eye contact with Taye.

I lay next to Taye and kissed her shoulder. I peeled the strap of her bra off of her shoulder, and ran my tongue down her arm. Taye rolled on her side, and I quickly unhooked her bra with one hand, while the other roamed freely across her flesh.

As Taye uncovered her breasts, I continued to feast on her skin with my tongue and hands, until I reached her feet. Damn. She even had pretty feet.

I took Taye's right foot in my hands, and began to massage the sole of her foot. I couldn't help but notice the glazed-over look in Taye's eyes, as I carefully and meticulously massaged her foot, before raising it to my lips. With her eyes wide open, and squirming because she's just a bit ticklish, Taye watched me suck and tongue each of her toes, and massage her calf. After a while, Taye could take no more. She grabbed me by the hand and pulled me to her. She unbuckled and took off my pants.

I stood before her naked and hard. Taye reached out and touched it, ran her hand across the length of it. "Thank you," she seemed to be saying at its size. "I hope you know how to use it," she said in a whisper.

I crawled onto the bed next to Taye, and our lips met again. Only this time, it was like we were on fire as our tongues darted feverishly in and out of each other's mouths. The shit was fucking intense.

Taye lay in my arms kissing me passionately, and stroking my erection. I closed my eyes and got lost in the sensation of her hands, and then the sensation of her lips—soft and wet—against my chest. Taye kissed and tongued her way down to my now throbbing hardness.

When she straddled my face and I inhaled her scent, my lips and tongue were engaged with her lips and clit, slowly tonguing her lips and sucking lightly on her clit. With my eyes closed, relying only on my senses of touch and smell, each seemed heightened. I felt Taye move, and the sensation of my sucking her lips gave way to the feeling of her soft wetness, slowly sliding up and down on my erection.

Taye moved her body slowly up and down, and then in circles. She reached for the bottle of lotion on the nightstand and poured it across my chest. She began to rub it in with her fingertips. Once she had covered my chest, she leaned forward and kissed me. She moved from side to side, rubbing her nipples across my chest in rhythm with the music.

I gotta be honest. The sensation I felt when her nipples rubbed against mine was indescribable. I grabbed her ass and ran my hands up and down her back, and across her cheeks. Taye started to move her hips faster; then she sat up and went to work. After a while, she stopped and moved her legs so her feet were on the bed.

I pushed harder, and I felt Taye's body begin to shake. Her eyes opened wide. She grabbed my shoulders and dug her nails in. Her mouth opened and she screamed, "You're gonna make me come!" then collapsed on my chest.

For the next half-hour or so, I held Taye close to my chest while she caught herself. As we lay in each other's arms, we talked about how off-the-chain the love we had just made was, and marveled over the anticipation of what was to come between us.

We were married the following year in a small, but intimate ceremony, and Taye was pregnant six months after that. During the first weeks of her pregnancy, she felt fine. Her appetite was good, and she got enough sleep. It was about the eighth week of her pregnancy when she started having cramps, and her stomach would have spasms.

When she consulted with her gynecologist, she was told that maybe she should change her diet. Something she may be eating wasn't agreeing with her. So, that's what Taye did. She started to eat more fruits and vegetables, and drinking more water. But the cramps didn't subside. In fact, they got worse. Just after her first trimester, she miscarried.

"I'm thinking that you're either stressed out, or just doing too much at work. I would think about taking some time off and relaxing. Working all day may not be good for you right now," the doctor said to her.

"Does this mean that I can't have any children?" she asked.

"Not at all. You're perfectly healthy, otherwise. Give your body a rest for about twelve weeks, and you and your husband can start on your family again." I took her hand and kissed it while she cried.

After Taye had gone for a checkup, three months later, and everything looked fine, we tried again. She made it through the first trimester. Taye was feeling great. She had taken a leave of absence from work, and was doing what the doctor ordered—getting lots of rest.

Six months into her pregnancy, Taye began to feel tightness in her stomach. It was like something was pulling it down, she told me. While we were lying in bed one night, she felt wetness between her legs. "Taye, you're bleeding!" I yelled.

Taye panicked, while I called 9-1-1. The ambulance was there in a matter of minutes and transported her to the hospital, but it was too late. The baby was stillborn.

After we lost the baby, Taye had gone into an extremely depressed state. All my attempts to talk to her about losing the baby, or anything for that matter, were met with complete silence, and the most distant stare. Our doctor told us that Taye was going through postpartum depression.

"Postpartum depression is a serious illness that generally occurs in the first few months after childbirth. It can also happen after miscarriage and stillbirth. Taye has all the symptoms: sadness, fatigue, insomnia, appetite changes, reduced libido, crying episodes, anxiety, and irritability, as she grapples with this devastating experience."

"Can you give her something for it?" I asked.

"I can prescribe an antidepressant for her, which in most cases, effectively relieves symptoms of postpartum depression for most women. However, I strongly recommend that you seek counseling for both you and Taye. A form of counseling called Cognitive-Behavioral Therapy has proved to be as effective as antidepressant medicine for postpartum depression."

But Taye wasn't interested in taking any antidepressant or counseling. "I'm not crazy," she said when the doctor suggested it. She did allow him to prescribe some sleeping pills to help with the insomnia.

After a while, Taye basically stopped speaking to me unless she had to. For months, she was cold, direct, and very much to the point. When she did speak, it was only because it was absolutely unavoidable. And sex . . ., well, nights that were once filled with great sexual experiences shared by two people who were desperately in love with each other, were now a distant memory. I kept trying—begging really. The times Taye did break down and open her legs, was just pity pussy.

"All right, all ready. Just come on and get it," she'd say.

No romance, no foreplay, just come on and get it. Then, she'd rush me—and I hated to be rushed. I had always been the type of lover that liked to take my time, savor each and every second of the pleasure. But now, it was hit it and quit.

"And I'm tired of that shit," I yelled at her one night after another round of unsatisfying sex. After that, Taye engrossed herself into her work, and dismissed any and all intimacy with me.

Finally, after months of me talking it up, Taye went to see a psychoanalyst so she could begin to work through her issues. The doctor told me that Taye's condition wasn't simply postpartum depression. She was suffering with a bipolar disorder. "The cause of bipolar disorder is not entirely known. Genetic, neurochemical, and environmental factors probably interact at many levels to play a role in the onset and progression of bipolar disorder," Dr. Larrieux told me at our first meeting. "The current thinking is that this is a predominantly biological disorder that occurs in a specific part of the brain, and is due to a malfunction of the neurotransmitters."

"And this happened because she lost a baby?"

"A biological disorder of this type may lie dormant and be activated spontaneously, or it may be triggered by stressors in life. A life event may trigger a mood episode in a person with a genetic disposition for bipolar disorder. Although no one is quite sure about the exact cause, bipolar disorders tend to be familial; meaning that it runs in families. About half the people with bipolar disorder have a family member with a mood disorder, such as depression. Your wife did mention that she had an aunt that suffered from depression."

This time, Taye agreed to the treatment option. But she didn't like the way the medication made her feel, so she stopped taking it. The sessions with Dr. Larrieux proved to be helpful. In time, Taye became a bit more interactive, and generally seemed a lot happier with herself, and our marriage, and she began to come to grips with the death of our second child. However, that generally happier feeling had no positive effect on our sex life.

Still, I was very happy when Taye came home and told me that Dr. Larrieux suggested she take some time off from work, and that we go away together.

"Some place romantic, is what she said, but I don't know about all that," Taye said to me that day.

"Why not?" I asked excitedly. I thought it was about time she suggested something constructive. "*Considering what we pay her,*" I started to say, but thought better of it. "I think that's a great idea. I'll even do the research for it."

A day later, I came home with pamphlets of Puerto Rico.

"Puerto Rico?" Taye asked. "I've never been to Puerto Rico."

"Then let's go." I got down on my knees and pleaded. "Let's

do something spontaneous. Something we'll both remember for the rest of our lives together."

"All right, I guess," she unenthusiastically responded.

So it was set. Taye and I were going to San Juan, Puerto Rico, to have fun together in the sun.

I hoped.

Chapter Two

Avonte

When I walked out of the airport in San Juan, Puerto Rico, I immediately had to dig in my purse for my sunglasses. During the four-hour flight from New York, I had three vodka and orange juices, and the San Juan sun was too much for me. I had come to San Juan to make some decisions about how the rest of my life was going to go. Since I was making life decisions, really heavy stuff, and since the temperature in New York was in the single digits, I decided that I wanted to be some place with sun.

The cab driver, a real cutie that spoke very little English, took me to the San Juan Marriott Resort and Stellaris Casino. After I checked in, I arranged with the concierge to have my luggage taken to my room, while I went down to the La Isla Grill and Pool Bar, and ordered another drink. "Kettle One and orange juice; and let me see a menu," I told my bartender as soon as he dropped the napkin in front of me. I'd been drinking cheap vodka on the plane, and my stomach was paying the price.

The bartender placed my drink and a menu in front of me. Then he promised to remember me, and have a drink ready for me next time I did my drinking poolside. I assured him that by the time I left, we would be the best of friends. My plan was to spend a lot of time drinking. Liquor has a way of focusing, or I should say intensifying, whatever it was I was thinking about. I wasn't planning on getting drunk, but I truly planned on staying fucked up.

The bartender, whose name was Manuel, and I chatted while I looked over the menu. Once I told him what I wanted to eat, he left me to do my drinking in peace. I gazed aimlessly at the pool, looking at what appeared to be nothing but couples having fun. Not that I was there to try and get with somebody, but damn, if I wanted to, it would have to be with one of the locals. And that wasn't happening. Then I saw this fine-ass brother walking by the pool. Now, I could get with him, but he was with somebody. I turned around on my stool and looked at the beach. The view was breathtaking. I had chosen wisely. I just had to get out of New York for a while, and away from my husband Tyrone.

Tyrone and I met my freshmen year at Syracuse. He was a career student, and at that time, he was working on his second masters. His first was in economics, the second one was in finance. It was my second day on campus, and I was trying to get adjusted to life out of my parent's house. We met in line at the cafeteria. He was in line behind me. I was about to reach for something, I don't remember what, but he stopped me. "You don't wanna eat that," Tyrone said.

"Why not?" I asked, and put it on my tray anyway, wondering

who this man was, and why he was trying to tell me what I should eat. But it was my second day, and I thought it was inappropriate for the around-the-way-girl from the Bronx to come out.

"I can see that you're new here," he said.

"Sure am."

He leaned close to me and whispered, "The food here is terrible. I never eat here," Tyrone said, and I noticed that he didn't have a tray. "You should let me take you to lunch."

I thanked him very much for the invitation, but told him that I would have to take a rain check. After all, I didn't know him from a can of paint, and I was not about to go anywhere with him.

"Are you sure?"

"Yeah," I said, and paid for my food.

"Well, my name is Tyrone Petrocelli."

"Avonte Braxton."

"It's good to met you, Avonte. That's a very pretty name for a very pretty lady."

"Thank you," I said graciously, and kept it moving, hoping that he wouldn't become a pest, and I'd have to call security.

"I'm sure I'll see you around," Tyrone said. Then he saw some guys he knew and went off with them.

After that, I saw Tyrone around campus from time to time. Anytime he saw me he'd come over and speak. We'd chat about how classes were going for me, and he'd invite me out to eat with him. I would always decline his invitation with some excuse about classes, or the need for more time in the library to study—which was true. Less party, more study. It's not that he wasn't a nice guy or that I was dating anybody else. I just never dated a white guy before. And it wasn't because he wasn't fine as hell for a white boy. He looked kind of like Brad Pitt.

By sophomore year, Tyrone had worn me down, and I agreed to go out to dinner with him. When he picked me up at my dorm in a white Lamborghini Diablo convertible, I thought I would faint. Over dinner and drinks, Tyrone told me that his father was in the shipping business, which he, at the time, thought was the most boring thing in the world–something he had no interest in whatsoever.

I had fun with Tyrone that night. Those years I always did. We went out a few more times before I finally agreed to come to his apartment for late-night cocktails. I knew what that meant and I was ready. Truth be told, that night, I was more than ready.

It didn't take long after we got there for things to start happening. As soon as the door closed, we were all over each other. Tyrone turned me around and began kissing the back of my neck, and squeezing my breasts. Then he lifted my dress and leaned me over the table. Tyrone quickly took off my panties and entered me. It took some wiggling on my part, but soon he was deep inside me, moving his hips. I rocked my hips until I had him where he could hit my spot right. Tyrone squeezed my breasts as he moved in and out of me. I closed my eyes because it was feeling so damn good. I looked over my shoulder at Tyrone taking off his shirt, all the while pounding away.

Then, Tyrone abruptly pulled out of me. When I turned to face him, he took me in his arms, kissed me, and then he picked me up. I wrapped my legs around his waist and held on tightly. He kissed me again, and we stumbled into the wall as he tried to carry me into the bedroom. He pinned me against the wall, and kissed and sucked my neck and breasts.

My fingers dug into his back when he pushed himself inside me again. We were going at it so hard that after a while, both of struggled to breathe. Tyrone took me in the bedroom. I unzipped my skirt, and it fell to the floor. My stiffened nipples were popping out of my lace semi-cup. I stepped out of my dress and joined him in the bed.

I lay there next to him, not believing how hung he was. Every time he sexed me, I had to fight the overwhelming urge to explode as soon as he entered me. And when I couldn't, Tyrone would drop between my thighs and try to sop every drop of my juices.

I knelt down on the bed because I love being taken from behind. Tyrone grabbed my hips again, and trusted himself deep inside me, finding my spot once more. My mouth dropped open, my eyes bucked, and I let go a gut-wrenching scream. When my body trembled from the pleasure, I knew he felt my warmth overflowing. I was in ecstasy.

We dated for the remainder of the year, until he received his masters in finance. He left Syracuse, and reluctantly, went to work for his father. We stayed in touch and would visit each other during my junior year. That was the year his father died, and suddenly, he was the chairman of the board. As you could imagine, I didn't see Tyrone much after that, but when we did, the sex was great. We still talked almost daily. He would tell me how much he hated running the company, and about how cutthroat it was in corporate America.

The day that I graduated, Tyrone was there, and I introduced him as a good friend to my parents. I didn't think my father needed to know that I'd been dating a white boy for the last three years. My father shook hands with Tyrone.

"Congratulations," he said to him, thinking that he, too, had just graduated.

"Thank you, sir," Tyrone said.

"What is your degree in?"

Tyrone smiled. "I have a master's in economics, and another in finance, but I graduated last year. I'm in the shipping business now, sir."

"What do you do in shipping?" my mother asked Tyrone.

"I'm the chairman of the board, actually."

"Oh" was all my mother could say.

"Did you say you were the chairman of the board?"

"Yes sir. I lost my father recently, and I had to step in and run the company."

"Which he hates," I threw in.

"Actually, Avonte, I'm starting to get into it," Tyrone said, and put his arm around me and I almost fainted; but it was about to get deeper than that very soon.

"Well, thank you for coming out to see our girl walk," my father said. "If you are looking for a English major with a lot of drive and initiative, that's your girl."

"I know that, sir. I'm sure that Avonte will make an excellent addition to anybody's staff. But I was hoping that she would be interested in accepting a different position."

"What position is that?" I wanted to know.

We had talked many times over the years about what I wanted to do when I graduated, but he never mentioned anything about a job at his company. Since we really weren't seeing each other on a regular basis, I had naturally assumed that he had moved on to somebody new, and I was just an occasional convenience. So I was surprised that he even showed up. And now he was about to offer me a job. Making big money, I hoped.

Tyrone looked at me, and then at my parents, before turning back to me. "I want to marry you, Avonte. Would you be my wife?"

So there my parents were, two simple black folks from the Bronx, and this rich white man just asked if he could marry their daughter. Needless to say, they were in shock, and so was I. I truly didn't see that coming.

I stood there speechless, truly not believing the words that came out of Tyrone's mouth. My father looked at me. "Avonte!"

"Huh?"

"Ain't you gonna answer the man?" my mother asked.

"Would y'all excuse us for a minute? I need to talk to Tyrone," I said, grabbing Tyrone by the hand and leading him anyway from my parents.

"Did you just ask me to marry you?"

"Yes Avonte. I love you, and I want to marry you. Do you want me to get down on one knee?" And then he actually started to do it.

I grabbed him before he got down there. "No."

He reached in his pocket, took out a ring box and handed it to me. I excitedly opened the box to reveal a platinum engagement ring with the biggest diamond I'd ever seen. He took the box from me and took the ring out of the box. He took my left hand and eased the ring on my finger. "What do you say, Avonte? Will you marry me?"

There was no way I was taking that ring off my finger, nor was I going to refuse to marry a millionaire. "Of course I will. I mean, the ring fits and all," I said, and held out my hand.

"Right; and it looks so good on your beautiful hand," Tyrone said, and kissed it.

That was five years ago, and during that time, we had what I considered, a very happy marriage. One filled with great sex, travel around the world, and of course, there was the money. Lots and lots of money; and I loved having money.

But all that changed about six months ago. Tyrone started spending more time at work and less time with me. "We are right in the middle of a major acquisition—one that will make us a much stronger company. I know you're not happy about this, but once it's a done deal, I promise to make it up to you, darling." He was right. I wasn't happy about it, but I had no choice but to except it.

I rolled along, finding new things to occupy my time. I even volunteered for this charity and that charity, but then Tyrone came home one day and said we needed to talk. I joined him in the living room, and sat down of the couch. Tyrone chose to stand.

"What do you want to talk about?" I asked.

"I want a divorce."

Just like that.

"What? What did you just say?" I asked, as the tears began to well in the corners of my eyes.

"I want a divorce."

Then Tyrone had the nerve to tell me that he had met somebody, and that he was in love with her. "Well, I didn't just meet her. She's an executive with the company we just acquired. We've been working very closely on the deal, and it just happened."

I couldn't believe my ears.

"I know this is sudden, and I'm sorry," Tyrone said, and walked away.

"That's it?" I yelled through my tears. "You waltz in here and tell me that you met somebody and you want a divorce. What about me? What about how I feel?"

"If it's money you're worried about, you know you'll be taken care of. You'll never have to worry about that," Tyrone said coldly, and left the house.

Before we got married, Tyrone asked me to sign a prenuptial agreement, and I agreed, but that wasn't the point. I loved and needed Tyrone, not his money.

I ran to the door behind him. I wanted to stop him—try to talk him out of it. Even though I didn't love him when we got married. I thought maybe it was for the money, but over the years, I had come to love and depend on him. I opened the door just in time to see him pulling out of the driveway, with some blonde in what was *my* spot.

I slammed the door and ran upstairs. I threw myself across the bed and cried until I had no more tears. Once I had cried myself out, I fell asleep, praying that when I woke up, it would be morning, and this would have all been a bad dream. But when I woke, Tyrone wasn't lying next to me, and I knew it was all too real.

I spent the better part of the day crying and drinking. That day, I wanted to get drunk. I didn't want to feel a thing. But after a while, when the bottle was empty, I began thinking about what I was gonna do. I didn't really read the prenup before I signed it—a foolish move on my part. But when Tyrone said that he loved me, and would never even think about leaving me, I signed the paper.

It was then that I decided I needed to get away for a while. So I called my travel agent and booked my trip. The rest of my life began that morning, and I was going to have to begin living it.

Chapter Three

Devin

When the Captain made the call to board the ship, I got my gear and followed the other men onto the ship for a day of deep-sea fishing.

As the ship headed out to sea, I took a moment to marvel at the fact that things had played out exactly the way I hoped they wouldn't. As soon as we got to the hotel and checked into our room, Taye started trippin'.

The bellman opened the door, brought in our bags, and put them down. "Will there be anything else?"

"No, everything is fine," I said, and handed the guy a tip.

Taye stood in the doorway. "This is totally unacceptable," she said, looking at the queen-sized bed.

"What's wrong, baby?"

"The bed. I requested a king-sized bed."

The bellman apologized and left the room promising to do what he could to rectify the situation. After thirty minutes, I wished that I had left the room with him. Taye spent all of that time complaining about everything: from the size of the room to the color of the drapes; from the view from the balcony to the fact that we hadn't seen any other black people since we got off the plane. "And what the hell is taking them so long to find another room," she fussed. She immediately picked up the phone and started blasting the front desk clerk.

As for me, I sat quietly in a chair by the sliding glass door to the balcony. I thought the view, which overlooked the pool, was excellent. And I enjoyed watching all of the well-tanned female bodies lounging by the pool.

Before I left New York, I had resolved myself not to buy into Taye's mood swings, and to have a good time regardless of what was going on with her. However, my hope was that Taye would let go of some of the things that seemed to constantly stress her out, and relax for change. She was always so uptight. In my mind, I pictured us having fun at the beach. Holding hands while we took long, romantic walks together. We would once again share little jokes that nobody understood but us. I really hoped that we would rekindle that magic that we once shared.

I looked at my wife as she wandered around the room, bitching and moaning about everything, including the fact that she should have gotten a pedicure before she left. And I knew in my heart, that was not going to be the case. I needed this vacation, and I be damned if I was going to allow Taye to ruin it for me.

Once we were taken to our new room with a king-sized bed, things got no better. At dinner that evening, she complained about the service and that her food was cold when it arrived, and kept it up throughout the meal.

"Really, baby? My food is fine," I said with a smile.

"What are you smiling about? I don't see anything funny here,"

Taye answered.

I put down my knife and fork, and then wiped my mouth with the napkin before placing it gently on the table. "Did you ever think that maybe, just maybe, if you hadn't given the waiter such a hard time, that he might have taken the time to re-warm your food before he brought it out?"

"Devin James, if that isn't the stupidest thing I've ever heard, I don't know what is."

"Trust me, Taye. I worked my way through law school waiting tables. And believe me, people like you get bad service on purpose."

With that, Taye stood up, slammed her napkin down on the table, and walked away.

"Taye! Taye!" I said loudly, and watched Taye walk out of the restaurant.

I signaled for the waiter and paid the check, but when I got outside, Taye was nowhere in sight. I walked around the area for a few minutes looking for her, before finally saying, "Fuck it." I got in a cab and went back to the hotel.

When I got back to the room, I found Taye in bed with her sleeping pill bottle and a half-empty glass of water on the nightstand. "God-damn sleeping pills," I said softly, as I looked at my watch. "It's too fuckin' early to go to bed."

I walked out of the room slamming the door behind me, and went downstairs to the hotel bar and got quietly drunk.

The next day wasn't any better for us. When I woke up, she was already gone and stayed gone, until well past nine that night. When she came back in the room, Taye had an armful of bags.

"Where were you all day?"

"I did some shopping, and then I went sightseeing," Taye said.

"You could have waited for me. Did you ever think that maybe

I wanted to go sightseeing?"

"If that were the case, you wouldn't have gone out last night and gotten so drunk that you couldn't get up. And don't even try to say that you didn't. I could smell the liquor on you a mile away."

"Baby, why does it have to be like this? All I want is for us to have a good time. I didn't come here with you for us to take separate vacations."

"Then maybe you should take some time and think about somebody other than yourself," she shouted, and went into the bathroom and slammed the door.

When she came out of the bathroom thirty minutes later, with nothing on but a towel, I was stretched out on the bed watching television. As Taye dropped the towel, I looked at my wife's beautiful body, and felt a twinge in my manhood.

Thoughts of making love to her ran through my mind. I thought if I apologized for being inconsiderate and sounded sincere doing it, if I spent some time and talked real nice to her, maybe she would allow me to make love to her. But those thoughts quickly flew out the sliding glass door when she reached for her sleeping pills.

At that moment, I considered going back downstairs to the bar and getting drunk again. I remembered hearing about a deep-sea fishing cruise I wanted to go on, but I knew Taye wouldn't be interested in anything like that, so I put the thought out of my mind. I had other ideas as I watched my wife put on her nightgown, slide under the covers, and turn her back to me with her ass poked out for me to kiss.

The cruise was scheduled to leave at seven in the morning, so I set the alarm for five-thirty and turned out the lights, mentally preparing for my twelve-hour cruise.

It was four hours out, four hours at sea, and four hours back, so by the time I finished telling big fish stories with the guys, and returned the fishing gear I had rented, it was almost ten.

When I stepped in the hotel lobby, I saw a very pretty lady walking barefoot, wearing a white-and-black thong bikini, turning men's heads—and some women's—in her wake. As I watched her walk, I thought about Taye's refusal to let me play on her playground. From where I stood, that woman had the kind of playground that I could get used to.

I started to follow her out to the pool to talk to her—she was just that fine. But then I looked at how I was dressed, and how I smelled after a day of fishing in the hot sun. *You smell like you work in a sushi bar,* I thought. I walked as quickly as I could to the elevator, and went back to my room.

When I got to the room, much to my surprise, and disappointment, Taye was still awake. "Where have you been all day?" Taye asked.

"Hello, Taye," I said. "I went on a deep-sea fishing cruise. How was your day?"

"Fine," was her single word answer, and then she returned her eyes and attention to the movie she was watching.

Without another word, I quickly retrieved my swimming trunks from my suitcase, and headed for the shower. Once I was showered and dressed, I grabbed a towel and headed for the door. "I'm going to take a dip in the pool. You wanna join me?" I asked, knowing what her answer would be.

"No, I'm watching a movie."

"Okay babe. You enjoy." And with that, I was out the door. I ran down the hall to the elevator, hoping that the woman wouldn't be gone when I got to there. But if she was gone, I would take a dip. And since Taye was still up and appeared to be in a good mood, I would go back to the room and try to make nice with the wife.

When I arrived at the pool, I looked around for her. "Damn!" I said out loud, disappointed that she was gone. I turned around to put my towel on a chair near the swallow end of the pool. As I turned to get in the water, she literally exploded from the water like Halle Berry did in that Bond movie.

Her head drifted back, and she ran her fingers through her wet hair, before opening her eyes. The beauty had the prettiest set of tits I had ever seen. Her nipples were protruding through the material like they were begging to get sucked. When she got to the steps, I was standing on the edge of the pool, directly in front of her. "Hello," I said.

"Hi," she said excitedly.

"How's the water?" I asked, and noticed the ring on her finger.

"Absolutely wonderful; but don't take my word for it. I think you should get in the water and see for yourself," she said with the prettiest smile.

"I think I will," I said, and laughed a little.

"So what are you waiting for?"

"Nothing," I said, and made my way to the steps.

"Coward," the beauty said. "Just get in," she challenged.

With that, I walked down to the deep end and tried to do the perfect dive. The water was cold at first, but I quickly got use to it and swam to the shallow end where the beauty was still standing.

"What do you think? Is this water wonderful or not?" Avonte asked.

"Yes, it is."

"I wouldn't steer you wrong," the beauty said, then went underwater. Then she came up for air, closed her eyes, and ran her fingers through her wet hair. I felt my dick getting hard. Damn, she was fine as hell. "My name is Avonte Petrocelli."

"Devin James," I said, and held out my hand.

"Are you enjoying yourself?" Avonte asked as she made her way back to me.

"Yeah," I answered slowly, "I'm having a good time."

"Hmm. Then why don't I believe you?"

"I don't know. Why don't you believe me?"

"Something about the look on your face, and the totally unconvincing way you said yeah." Avonte licked her lips.

I had to laugh a little, but chose not to comment on her statement; especially since it was the truth. "What about you, Avonte; are you having a good time?" I asked, and hoped she would lick her lips like that again.

"Oh, yeah, I'm having a great time. Mostly, I've been out here working on my tan."

"You tan well. Like a bronze goddess, Avonte."

"Well, thank you," Avonte said and smiled. That was nice, too, but not as nice as her tongue floating over her lips.

I took a step back from Avonte and went under the water. When I opened my eyes in the pool, I got an eyeful of Avonte's wide hips, and the luscious mound between her legs. When I came back up for air, Avonte was walking away from me. As she got out of the pool, Avonte turned her head and winked at me.

"I'm sure I'll see you around, Devin," she said, as she walked off dripping wet.

"Oh, yeah, Ms. Avonte, I'm sure that you'll see me around."

I wasn't ready to go back to the room after Avonte left, so I swam around in the pool, thinking how peaceful it was. I thought about how I wanted to be in there with Taye. She used to love the water. Weekend trips to the beach was our thing; or at least one of them. Now, the way things were looking, she wouldn't even go to the beach with me.

The longer I swam, I slowly came to the conclusion that if I was going to have a good time on my vacation, it would be by myself. It wasn't how I wanted it to be, but like I said, I would be damned if I let her ruin things for me. But then I thought maybe I was overreacting. Maybe when I get back to the room, Taye and I could go out and experience nightlife in San Juan. Maybe she'd even go to the casino with me, but that would be pushing it. Taye hated smoke-filled casinos, even before everything happened.

With a brand new attitude, I got out of the pool, dried off, and headed back to the room. Dancing. *Taye used to like dancing to Latin music,* I thought as I put my keycard in the door. "Taye," I called as walked in, and immediately knew that salsa dancing the night away wasn't gonna happen.

Taye was fast asleep. The movie she was watching was now watching her. I went and sat down on the bed next to her. "Taye," I said, and shook her gently. "Wake up, baby. Let's go do something."

But she didn't answer. Taye was dead to the world, and the reason was there on the nightstand: her bottle of sleeping pills. Once she popped a couple of them, Taye could sleep through an earthquake. I got up from the bed and went and sat out on the balcony for a while. It was a beautiful night, and I wasn't about to spend it in the room watching Taye sleep. I got up and got in the shower, got dressed, and got out of there.

I went to the concierge's desk and asked for a cab. Once I was in the cab and the driver asked me where I wanted to go, I told him I didn't know. "I was hoping that you could tell me."

"What do you want to do, *señor?*" he asked in better English than I expected. "You look for *mujeres?*"

"*Mujeres?*"

"Women, *señor*," he smiled, and cupped his hands in front of his chest.

"No, no. Where's a good place to go dancing?" I asked.

"Rumba."

"Yeah, rumba," I said, thinking he was talking about the dance.

"No, no, *señor*. Rumba is a club in old San Juan."

"Oh." I felt stupid, but fuck it, I'm on vacation.

"I tell you, *señor*, the club is small and it gets crowded, but it's known in San Juan's underground nightlife circuit as one of the places to go. They film many crowd scenes for *Dirty Dancing: Havana Nights* there."

"Really?"

"*Sí, señor.*"

"That's where I want to go," I told him. And before long, I was at Rumba. It was packed just as my driver said it would be. I looked around the spot, wishing one more time that Taye had been awake to come with me. I went to the bar and ordered a drink. "Barcardi 151," I called out to the bartender. When he handed it to me, I quickly drained the glass, grabbed the first woman that walked by, and took her out on the dance floor.

While I was out there doing my thing, I happened to look around and became excited when I saw Avonte dancing her ass off. She was wearing a flowing white sleeveless dress that tied around the neck, and fell right into those tits I had admired earlier.

I watched her while she danced. She had the prettiest smile and eyes that drew me to her like a bee to honey. When she left the dance floor, I quickly thanked the woman I was dancing with, and went after Avonte. I had never cheated on Taye. The idea never even crossed my mind. Aside from the fact that we hadn't been having sex on a regular basis, I really loved my wife—even though, lately, she'd been making my life a living hell. All that changed the moment I saw Avonte walk through that lobby. Since that moment, I hadn't been able to think of anything else.

She went to the bar and I walked up behind her. "Hello again, Avonte."

She turned around quickly when she heard my voice. "Well, hello, Devin."

"You look like you're enjoying yourself."

"I am. Having a ball," Avonte said, and turned to the bartender. "Kettle One and orange juice." She turned to me. "What are you drinking?"

"Barcardi 151," I told her over the music, leaning close.

When she handed me my drink, I moved closer to her, and once again, I felt the heat of her body. And once again, it caused the same effect.

"Come dance with me," Avonte said when a new song began.

I followed Avonte out on the floor, our drinks in hand. We finished our drinks on the dance floor, discarded our empty glasses on the nearest table, and kept dancing. We stayed out there for a long time. Avonte was quite the salsa dancer. We were smiling and laughing and having a good time. By the time we left the floor, we were both drenched.

We went back to the bar and I ordered another round of drinks.

While we drank, we talked about the time we had just spent on the dance floor. Then I asked the question that I had wanted to ask her since I'd first seen her. "Did you come here by yourself tonight?"

"Yes."

"Where's your husband?" I asked.

"I was about to ask you the same question." Avonte laughed.

"Yeah, but I asked you first."

"To be honest with you, my husband is in New York."

"Is that where you live?" I asked, hoping she'd say yes.

"Yeah, we live in Glen Cove; out on the island."

"Oh really? I live in New York too."

Avonte smiled like it was the best news she'd heard all day. "Now, stop avoiding the question. Where's your wife?"

"She's in the room sleeping. I tried to wake her to see if she wanted to come, but I couldn't wake her."

"You must not have tried too hard."

"It's a long story."

"Have the two of you been having fun together?"

"No," I said flatly. "We're taking separate vacations, or at least that's how it seems. At this point, I've spent more time with you than I have with her."

By this time, Avonte was laughing. "I'm sorry to hear that, Devin. I'd ask you why that is, but I'm guessing that's a long story too."

"And you'd be right."

"Sorry, Devin, got no time for long, sad stories. Got one of my own I'm trying to work my way through."

"Maybe someday I'll tell you mine, and you can tell me yours."

"Pity party for two, huh? But that assumes that we'll get to know each other, and be comfortable enough to do that. I'm sure your wife won't like that."

I started to say that at this time of night, my wife doesn't even know I exist. "True, and I don't think your husband will be too happy with your new friend either."

Avonte looked away but then she turned back quickly. "Come on. Let's dance."

We spent the rest of the night dancing, drinking, and talking about any– and everything. When Rumba closed at four in the morning, we caught a cab back to the hotel. I walked proudly through the lobby, with Avonte on my arm like she was my wife. When we got to the elevator, Avonte turned and faced me. "I guess this is where we say good night."

"I was hoping you'd let me escort you to your room."

"I don't think that would be a good idea," Avonte said, and pressed the button for the elevator.

"Well, I guess this is good night then. I had a great time with you, Avonte. Best time I've had in a very long while."

"I was about to say the same thing. Thank you for showing a lady a good time."

Well, why does it have to end? I could come up to the room with you and knock your back out. That's what I wanted to say to her. "It was my pleasure." I held out my hand as the elevator door opened. "Good night, Avonte."

She took a step forward and kissed me on the cheek. "Good night, Devin." Avonte got on the elevator. "Maybe I'll see you tomorrow," she said as the door began to close.

"I don't think you'll be able to keep me away from you."

Chapter Four

Avonte

I leaned against the wall and took a deep breath. I had to get away from Devin before I changed my mind, dragged him to my room, ripped off his clothes, and rode him like a horse at the Kentucky Derby. It had been a very long time since I'd had something thick and stiff inside me. Since Tyrone started fucking his new blonde bitch, which I assumed began when they started working on the acquisition, I hadn't had any. Unless masturbation was considered getting some, it had been six months. I'm guessing the word *overdue* would have been an understatement at that point.

I had a good time with Devin. He was fun to be with, and a good dancer. While we were walking through the lobby, I looked at his hands and feet. *Big hands, big feet–big dick;* I know it's an old wives tale, but in my experience, it's held true. Devin had big feet–size thirteen or fourteen, if I had to venture a guess. And his hands were big, too. But he's a big guy–six-two and well-built, so on him, big hands and feet would only be natural.

I sat down on the bed and turned on the television. I had to remind myself that I didn't come here to get laid. I was here to relax, and to plan the rest of my life. But some serious fucking would have been nice right now. It's too bad that Devin was here with his wife. If he wasn't, I would have considered calling his room, and inviting him to come and play with me.

Several times while we were dancing and I turned my back to him, Devin would ease his body against mine. I felt him; felt how hard I was getting him. Nice to know I can still turn a man on. I stood up and got undressed in front of the mirror. "What does Blondie have that I don't?"

After a quick shower, I slid under the covers. Even though I'd been drinking all day and all night, and had been out dancing, I was too hyped about my night with Devin to go to sleep. I picked up the remote and began flipping channels, thinking that it would help me fall asleep. I turned to HBO and Real Sex was coming on. I liked Real Sex. Let's just say it's always very interesting, and leave it that.

With my eyes closed, I lay there listening to the opening music, and then I heard a woman moaning like she was getting the shit fucked out of her. It's Real Sex, so that didn't faze me. Then I heard this man say something about the monster, the intruder, and the hammer. But it was when he said that this machine will spin, stroke, and vibrate all at the same time, that I opened my eyes, because I had to see what he was talking about.

I opened my eyes to see this woman lying naked on a bed with her legs in the air. There was this machine in front of her. It had a large wheel with a rod attached to it, and a dildo attached to that. I sat in amazement watching this machine fuck this woman, thinking I have got to get me one of those, and I got turned on. Again. The shower calmed me down a bit, because Devin had me on fire. I thought about how we were dancing, and how he wrapped those strong arms of his around me. I felt good in his arms.

The longer I watched the more turned on I got. I turned off the television and pulled back the covers. I licked my lips and put two fingers in my mouth, and went searching for something to play with. My nipples were hard, so I pinched and squeezed them a little bit. It didn't take long for my pussy to start throbbing and for my hand to find its way down there. I took my fingers and spread my lips apart, and then I gently massaged my clit. I slid two fingers in and out of my sweet opening, slowly at first, but it never stays that way, and I thought about Devin.

By then, I was so wet that my juices are flowing freely out of me, slowly dripping between my butt checks. My pussy was on fire and my nipples were so damn hard, I had to give them some attention. I eased my wet fingers out and began squeezing my nipples. My nipples were wet with my juices, and I wished I had taken the time to get the bullet out of the bag. But I was too far-gone to even think about stopping to go get it. I stuck my fingers back inside myself and picked up the pace. Soon, my eyes and mouth were wide open, and I was screaming my ass off. If there was a better feeling on earth, I needed to know about it.

It was almost noon the following day when I finally opened my eyes. I slept really well, which didn't surprise me with the day I'd had, not to mention the way I finished it off.

As I made my way to the shower, I couldn't help but think

about Devin. We had a really good time dancing. More fun than I'd had in a long time. As I enjoyed the sensation of steaming, hot water against my skin, I thought about my life to this point. Sure, I'd traveled to parts of the world that I had always dreamed of. Tyrone's money allowed me to live a very comfortable life. I didn't want for anything. But suddenly, it occurred to me that my life was very safe, very structured. That was the way Tyrone wanted it.

It wasn't always that way. When we were dating in college, spontaneity was his middle name. It wouldn't be anything for him to say on a cold Friday night in January, "Hey, baby. It's too cold to spend the weekend here. Let's fly to Jamaica for the weekend."

But of course that was before his father died, and he took over the business. Everything changed at that point, and it changed him. Tyrone went from the wild and crazy guy I'd fallen in love with, to Mr. Structure, the king of discipline. I decided right then that in this new life that was being thrust upon me, things would be different. From this day forward, I was going to experience everything life had to offer. Take some risks.

"Have some fun!" I shouted at the top of my lungs.

Once I had my bikini on, and my hair and makeup just right, I went down to post up at the pool to people watch. I know, I know, posting up by the pool for yet another day didn't seem all that risqué, but you never can tell what might happen.

Just for a change of pace, I decided to have lunch in one the restaurants in the hotel. Even though it was after noon, I still wanted some breakfast food. A lot of people think that it's taboo to eat breakfast food after noon. My soon-to-be ex-husband was one of them, but I was living on the wild side from here on out, so what the fuck!

A funny thing happened to me while I was eating that afternoon. I realized that I was alone. It scared me at first because I had never been alone. I went from my parent's house to college, and then to Tyrone. I wondered was I ready for that; ready to make my own choices. In addition to drinking, I thought a lot about where my life had been, and where I wanted it to go.

And that was the problem. All I've been for years is Mrs. Petrocelli. Volunteering for this cause or the next, attending this function or that important fundraiser. I'd been to so many of those things I was starting to think my first name was, *and his lovely wife*. Now, that all was behind me. My name is Avonte, and unfortunately, beyond that, I didn't know very much about who I was.

When I got to the pool, the usual suspects that were there the day before were there again.

"Afternoon, Manuel," I said to my bartender as I sat down.

"How are you today, Miss Avonte," he said, then placed a bar napkin in front of me and handed me a menu.

"I feel great today." It wasn't too long after, that Manuel had my drink ready, and had sat it on the bar napkin. "I won't be needing a menu today. I ate in the Ocean Terrace."

When I said that I had eaten inside, the look on his face distorted. Like he was really hurt that I wouldn't be eating there. He dropped his head and went away without another word.

"Whatever," I said softly. I spun my chair around and looked out at the beach. As it had been the previous two days, the weather was beautiful, and the water was calm.

That's when I saw him. There was Devin, walking down the beach. And much to my surprise and sheer joy, he was alone. "Charge the drink to my room, Manuel," I said, and got up.

"I'm gonna have some fun."

I walked down to the beach and headed for Devin, and I had to hurry just to catch up with him. I started to call his name, but two things stopped me. One, wifey may be around, and two, it would be just too ghetto.

While I followed behind Devin, wondering where he was going, I considered inviting him up to my room to finish the job I had imagined him doing before I drifted off to sleep. But then I thought that I'd like to have some fun today. "What? Fucking ain't fun?" I asked myself. It is, but I'd been in San Juan for two days, and other than going to Rumba the night before, I hadn't been anywhere.

Today, I wanted to play tourist. I wasn't really all that interested in going on any kind of sightseeing tour, but I wanted to see San Juan. Have an island adventure. And Devin's sexy-ass would make the perfect escort. "Hello, Devin," I said when I got close enough to him.

He turned around quickly and he smiled like seeing me was the best thing that ever happened to him. "Hey, Avonte!" he said, and ran back to me. "How are you doing today?" Devin asked, and devoured me with his eyes. "You look—" he started, but couldn't finish his sentence. Devin shook his head and finally said, "You are wearin' the hell outta that bikini."

I laughed a little and said, "Thank you, Devin. You're looking pretty nice in those trunks." And he was. The trunks were tight on him, and the longer he looked at me, the more the print of his dick became prominent.

"Thank you."

"So, I wasn't expecting to see you today. I just knew you and wifey had a romantic day planned."

Devin smiled at me, and I got a little wet.

"Yeah, well, to be honest with you, Avonte, I did have a romantic day planned. But when I woke up this morning, Taye was gone, again, and I haven't seen her all day."

"What's up with you guys anyway?"

"What do you mean?"

"Well, you said yesterday that you've spent more time with me than you have with her, and here we are again. So what's the deal?"

Devin took a deep breath, and then he told me his story. He went into this sad story about how they had lost two babies, and the effect that had on his wife and their marriage.

"I can't even imagine what that must feel like," I said, as we walked along the beach together. I don't know how far or how long we walked, because I enjoyed the conversation so much. Like everything else in my life, conversation, or more to the point, conversation with a man other than Tyrone, was nonexistent. Devin told me what he did for a living and where he worked. I purposely told him very little about myself. I felt like if I started talking about my life, that I would start to cry. "So, Devin, tell me about this romantic day you had planned for wifey?" I asked when we got back to the hotel.

"We're doing the first part of it. I had planned to take a walk along the beach, some good conversation, maybe play in the water. Then I was thinking about wandering around old San Juan. Maybe even hire a car and go out to the areas that most tourists don't see."

"You mean the stuff that you don't get on the packaged sightseeing tour?"

"Exactly." Devin smiled at me, and it had the same effect it had on me the last time. "Then after a fine meal, I wanted to top off the evening with a horse and buggy ride in the moonlight."

"Well, I may not be your wife . . ." I began.

"Taye."

Whatever. ". . . But, I'm not doing anything, and I would hate to see a great plan go to waste."

"You serious?"

"Don't I look serious?" I stopped and held out my arms for effect. Devin looked me over for a second or two longer than I thought he should.

"Avonte, you're a very serious woman."

"Give me a few minutes to change, and I'll meet you in the lobby," I told Devin.

"Sounds good."

After a quick change, I met Devin in the lobby. I looped my arm in my escort's arm, and we caught a cab to San Juan's Old City.

Even though I said I didn't want to, we took the walking tour. We walked behind the crowd. So far behind that we lost them at Fuerte San Felipe del Morro or El Morro Fortress. By the time we came out of the Cathedral de San Juan, we had lost the tour entirely. "I really did want to go to La Muralla."

"What's that?" Devin asked in a tone that let me know that he was less than enthusiastic about doing more sightseeing.

"La Muralla is the City Wall," I said all bright and bubbly. "It's a city by the bay that they built a wall around."

"Okay, let's go," Devin said, and checked his watch. We got directions and found our way along the curve of the bay that led to La Muralla. It was completed in 1782 to protect the city against enemy attacks.

At that point, I had done enough walking for one vacation, so we went for drinks at a little place called La Bombonera. Devin and I talked for hours while we drank and dined on rice with squid, roast leg of pork, seafood asopao, and pineapple pie for dessert.

The sun was going down when we left La Bombonera. Devin, as he'd done throughout the day, checked his watch. "Do you have to go?" I asked, hoping he'd say no, and wondering how far I was willing to take this with a married man.

I could tell by the way he talked about her that he still loved her. But she seemed to be pushing him away, driving a wedge between them. Along with his love I could feel his anger at her; anger for something that wasn't her fault. His wife made him feel unwanted. I knew what that felt like. I felt pretty unwanted, too. Maybe that's why I could feel his pain. It made me want him.

"Even if I did, I don't want to," Devin said.

"So, what should we do now?"

"How adventurous are you feeling, Avonte?"

"I'm ready for whatever—within reason, of course."

"Of course."

"So, what do you have in mind?"

"Come on," Devin said, and took me by the hand. We got in the first cab we could find. "Coliseo Gallistico," he said to the driver.

The driver let out a sneaky kind of laugh and drove on. "Where are we going, Coliseo—where?"

"What happened to your sense of adventure?"

"Okay, this is where the within reason part kicks in. See, I'm probably gonna be down for whatever we're going to do, but the common sense part of me, go figure, says you're in a foreign country with two men that you don't know very well. Maybe I should at least know where I'm going," I said sort of jokingly, but I was serious.

Devin inched a little closer to me in the backseat. "It's nothing illegal, and it's nothing sexual either. But it *is* violent, and some people find it distasteful."

"*Si, si,*" the driver agreed.

"But I assure you, Avonte, you'll be perfectly safe. And anytime you're ready to go, you just say the word."

And that seemed to hold me until we arrived at Coliseo Gallistico, and I realized that it was a cock-fighting arena. "Cock-fighting?" I asked with my hands on my hips. "You into this?"

"No. This will be my first time," Devin said, as we continued walking toward the door. "I wanted to do something different."

"Well, it's definitely that."

Devin stopped and turned to me. "If you don't want to go, I mean if it's too much for you, we don't have to go in. We can find someplace else to go. I just thought, you know, this kind of stuff you can't do in New York."

"'Cause it's barbaric, not to mention illegal."

"We don't have to go," Devin said and turned away.

I looked at him as we began walking away. His shoulders had dropped, and his once proud and confident walk that I found so sexy, had all but disappeared. He was really looking forward to doing this, just like I was all hyped about the Wall City. Now I felt selfish. And I wondered should I care.

I had decided back at the Cathedral de San Juan that I wasn't going to sleep with him tonight. We'll probably never see each other again. So do I really care if he's upset that I don't wanna see mindless violence masquerading as a sport?

The answer was no. But I'm not a selfish person and my opinion of me at this point, was much more important than what Devin thinks of me. So I stopped.

"Wait a minute, Devin."

"What?" he asked and sulked back to me.

"Come on." I looped my arm in his and began walking. "We're going to a cock-fight."

"You sure?"

"Yeah, I'm sure–sure I never wanna see that spoiled child look for the rest of the night."

"Was it that bad?"

I didn't bother commenting. The answer was obvious.

When we got inside the arena it was almost full, but still kind of quiet. We took our seats in time to watch the handlers as they teased the birds with a third bird, before teasing them with each other to make them more aggressive–I guess. All roosters were outfitted in white or blue ankle bands.

As the fight began, the roosters knew what to do. The atmosphere totally changed from the second the first bell sounded. People were shouting bets all across the arena. "Five hundred on *azul*!" *Azul* means blue in Spanish.

At first it was quite shocking, then it got a bit disgusting, but after a couple of matches, I was surprisingly into it. By the fourth match I was making bets, and during the match I was on my feet yelling at the top of my lungs, "*AZUL, AZUL, AZUL!*"

After ten matches, I had had enough and was ready to go. We took a cab back to our hotel, and Devin checked his watch. "What's that wife of yours gonna say when you drift in after midnight?"

"Nothing. We're leaving in the morning, so she'll probably be asleep when I get there. And if she's awake, I'll tell her that I went to the cock-fights. She'll say, fine, because that's her answer to just about everything when she's like this."

When the cab arrived, I walked through the lobby with Devin. But since I decided he wasn't getting any, I stopped at the elevator. I saw no point in tempting myself by saying good night at the door. "I think we should say good night here."

I had to laugh a little to myself, because the look on his face was priceless. It went from "I'ma tear that ass up" to total shock. Then confusion set in, like he was trying to figure out what he'd done wrong, to spoiled child. "I told you about that look."

"That bad?"

"It's worse this time."

"You just don't know."

I rolled my eyes. "Believe me, I do."

But a promise is a promise; especially to yourself. The solution to Tyrone cheating on me with Blondie was not to become a cheater myself. I had more pride in myself than that. But I wasn't stupid.

There was a man sitting by the elevator fooling with his laptop, and taking notes. *Poor guy, working on his vacation, at this hour.* "Excuse me, Devin."

I borrowed the man's pen and wrote down my cell phone number. "Call me some time. We'll have lunch, or whatever," I said, as the elevator door opened.

"Or whatever."

I got on the elevator. "Good night, Devin. I had a really good time hanging out with you."

Chapter Five

Qianna

Fresh outta Bedford Hills Correctional Facility for Women, and back in the city. The charge was aggravated assault. It wasn't my first time in jail. My first bid was at juvenile when I was fifteen. I came home one night from having sex with my boyfriend, and heard my mama screaming. I went in the apartment and saw my mama's drunk-ass man slappin' her in the face, while he raped her in the living room.

I jumped on his back and started hittin' him, you know, tryin' to get his drunk-ass off her. He got up off my moms and came after me. That bitch just laid there and watched that nigga beat my ass, and then he raped me, too. My own mom didn't do shit to help me.

After he was done with me, he left the house. My moms got up and came to me. I was cryin' and shit. She helped me get up. "You all right, Qianna?"

"He raped me, Mama," I yelled, and pushed her off of me. "Why the fuck didn't you help me?"

"What the fuck was I gon' do?" she said, and took me in the bathroom to clean me up. "No! We gotta call the cops!"

"No!"

"But he raped me, Mama!"

"No!" she yelled back at me. "We ain't callin' no damn cops."

"Why not?" I yelled through my tears.

"He didn't mean it. He just drunk, that's all. You know how he get when he like that. He don't mean us no harm."

I couldn't believe the shit that bitch was talkin'. That drunk-ass nigga beat and raped my mama. Then he did the same shit to me. And this bitch didn't wanna do shit about it.

I knew what I had to do.

The next night I waited until he was drunk again. Him and my moms was sittin' in the livin' room watchin' TV, like that shit never happened. Her on the couch; him in the chair. I went in the kitchen and got the biggest knife I could find. They were too into whatever bullshit show they was watchin' to pay me any mind. I came up behind him, grabbed his head, and slit his fuckin' throat. While my moms screamed her fuckin' ass off.

I had just killed a man, and you know what?

I liked it.

Got off on it.

Somehow ending his life began mine. I felt powerful and strong, like I could do anything, and nobody could stop me.

That was, until the cops came and took my ass to jail for murder. And do you know that bitch wouldn't testify for me at my trial? She told the cops that he never touched me, and he didn't rape either one of us. Stupid bitch, scared to death of a dead man.

On my second day at the juvenile facility, this big burly lookin' girl cut in front of me in the food line. I let that pass, 'cause I didn't give a fuck.

But I started paying attention to this bitch, seein' how she rolled. She had everybody in our buildin' scared to death of her. I stayed out of her way for the next couple of weeks. At the time, my thinkin' was, you know, mind your business, stay out of trouble, do your time and get out of there.

It didn't work out that way. Shit never fuckin' does.

Our next confrontation came in the cafeteria again, when she knocked my tray out of my hands.

"You shouldn't be so clumsy, bitch," she said to me.

"Who you callin' a bitch, bitch?" I said, and stepped to her. Then the poo-lice came and got between us.

"What's goin' on here?"

"She threw her tray at me," the bitch lied.

Not only did I have to clean up her mess, but since the bitch told them that I threw the tray at her, they took me to the detention unit. Might as well call it what it was—they threw my ass in the hole for two days.

I knew what I had to do.

When I got out and went back to my buildin', I played it cool, but I had a plan for that bitch. For the next few days, I walked around the yard, picking up rocks.

Once I thought I had enough, I put all the rocks in a sock and waited for my time. After lights out that night, I made my move to her bed with the sock full of rocks behind my back.

"What you want, bitch?" she asked when she looked up and saw me standing there.

"For you to die," I said, and beat her wit' it. I don't know how many times I hit her, but there was blood everywhere. Then I took her pillow and put it over her face until she stopped moving.

She was dead.

The feeling I got while I was killin' her was indescribable.

I went around to everybody and gave each one of them a rock, and told them to get rid of it. After that, I was the big bitch in the room. Now they were all scared to death of me. And nobody fucked wit' me for the rest of my bid.

When I got out, I thought I needed a change of scenery, so I went to California. I had been out there chillin' in LA for a couple of months. LA was nice, and I liked it out there. Anyway, one night I was buyin' some green, you know, to get my head right; and the mutha fucka cheated me on some weight.

"Yo, this shit light than a mutha fucka."

"That's an ounce, baby girl. I weighed it myself just 'fore you got here."

"Then your scale is broke. Why you tryin' to cheat me, nigga?"

"Fuck you, bitch. Take that shit and get the fuck out."

"Fuck that, nigga. Gimme my fuckin' money back."

"I ain't givin' you shit. You need to take what you got, and get the fuck outta here 'fore I kick your ass."

That's when I put my hand on my knife. "You ain't kickin' this ass. Not today."

"Fuck you, bitch," he said, and started toward me like he was gonna do something. I pulled out my blade and next thing you know, it was sticking in his chest.

"Fuck you!" I shouted.

I watched his dead body drop to the floor. Then I pulled my blade out of his chest and cleaned his blood off of it. I got the fuck outta there with the weed and my money, and was happy than a mutha fucka that we were alone.

Next time, I wasn't that lucky. Six months later, I was at a party and there were plenty of witnesses. I was there with my woman, and we got into it over her sweatin' this other bitch while I'm sittin' right there wit' her. That shit was just fuckin' disrespectful.

"What is you doin'?" I asked her.

"What?"

"You must see somethin' you want," I said, and got in her face.

"She is kinda cute," this bitch had the fuckin' nerve to tell me. Okay, the bitch was fine as hell, but that ain't the point.

"You want that bitch, gon' be wit' her then." I was so fuckin' mad I slapped the shit outta her.

Only problem was, my woman was also this dude's woman, so when I slapped her, he wanna do something about it.

His punk-ass come runnin' over there. "What the fuck is wrong wit' you, Qianna?"

"Mind your fuckin' business. This between me and her," I said, and stood up. I don't back down for no fuckin' body. So when that nigga got in my face, I stepped right to his chest. "You need to back the fuck up."

Well, you know how shit can go. He was pushin' me. I pushed him. When the nigga fucked around and slapped me, I took out my blade and swung it at him, but I missed. He rushed at me and my blade ended up in his gut. I was on the bus back to New York that next morning.

Chapter Six

Devin

It was Monday morning, and I was back at my desk. I worked as a tax attorney at the law firm of Weiss, Cabot & Davenport. The first day back from vacation was always the hardest, so I spent most of the morning moving the papers on my desk from side to side to give the appearance of work. My body was there, but in general, my mind was in Puerto Rico, totally focused on Avonte.

Now it was back to work.

The pile of mail seemed mountainous. "I'll deal with that later." I decided to check my voice mail. Before I left, I'd recorded a new message advising callers that I would be out of the office for the next three days, directing them to call Sandra Marshall. They didn't seem to care. There were forty-two new messages. The result was the same when I turned on my computer and logged into e-mail, and found ninety-four unread messages. I took a deep breath and spent the next three hours reading and answering e-mail, listening to voice mails and returning calls.

So far, the only thing I had going for me was that the morning meeting had been rescheduled until one o'clock. Every now and then, I would glance at Avonte's number. I picked up the phone and was about to dial her number when Sandra Marshall, my assistant, knocked on the door.

She and I worked well together. She was my right hand. Sandra moved to New York with her husband Ike, from San Antonio. She spoke with the most adorable southern accent, and had an almost childlike innocence about her. But Sandra was passionate when it came to things she believed in, and Chinese food. She was a pretty woman in a very natural kind of way. Her hair was shoulder length, parted down the middle. She dressed stylish, but not flashy; pants and a blouse every day. She was proud of the fact that the last time she wore a dress was six years ago. That was the day she interviewed for the job. The only makeup she wore was lipstick. "You busy?" she asked as she walked in and sat down.

"Trying my best not to be," I said.

"Hard to get back in it, ain't it? How was the vacation?"

"Sandra, let me tell you. We had a ball. The first couple of days, you know, we played the tourist role—went on all the tours. Did some shopping," I lied. "Yes, I brought you something. But I left it home."

"What'd you get me?" Sandra asked excitedly.

"I got you a bottle of Bacardi Rum and a Bacardi shirt. I'll try to remember it tomorrow."

"See that you do. So what else did you do?"

"Spent a lot of time at the beach."

"I can tell. You look darker. Ike and I went there for our honeymoon. I had a good time, but Ike hated it."

"Really? Why?"

"You'll have to ask him."

"I'll do that, if I ever get to meet him." We'd made plans to get together on several occasions, but something would always come up, or one couple or the other wouldn't be able to make it. We almost met at the company picnic last year, but we kept missing each other. "I'm starting to think he's a figment of your imagination. And that picture on your desk came with the frame."

"Trust me, Devin, he's very real," she said, in a way that made me curious.

"Sounds like trouble in paradise."

"Nah, nothing like that. I don't even feel like going into it."

"Okay, far be it for me to pry into your personal affairs."

Just then, Winston Hunter stuck his head in the door. "Good morning, Devin. Morning, Sandra."

"Morning, Winston," Sandra said, and got up.

"What's up, Winston?"

"Let me get to work," Sandra said, and started to leave my office.

"I didn't mean to run you off," Winston told her.

"You're not. I have a lot to do this morning," she said, and turned to me. "We can go over what happened while you were gone anytime you're ready," she commented, and left my office.

"How the was vacation?" Winston asked.

He and I were competing for partner at the firm. Typical blonde-haired, blue-eyed white boy who thought the world was his playground. But since he was the only guy there close to my age, Winston was my *at work* best friend.

"The vacation was fine. Had a good time," I said, and balled up Avonte's number, and tossed it in the trashcan next to my desk. "How have things been going around here?"

Winston started to bring me up to speed on all of the goings on at the office during my absence. But I wasn't listening. My mind was still on Avonte. I wanted Avonte bad. And I knew what calling her would mean. She'd made me feel excited and alive, you know, the way Taye used to. I looked at the picture of Taye on the corner of my desk. I loved Taye so much and had never cheated on her, but wondered how much more could I take.

I looked up at Winston, who had taken a seat, and was still going on about work. "So, did you and the Mrs. play nice together, or does a state of war still exist between the two of you?"

"Yeah, we got along okay," I lied.

"You know what, Devin, old buddy? It's a good thing that you're a tax attorney and not a trial lawyer."

"Why is that, Winston?"

"Because when you lie, it's written all over your face. So come on, old pal of mine . . . the truth this time."

"Okay, if you really must know. I had a good time. I drank more than I should have. I took a twelve-hour deep-sea fishing cruise. Did some swimming, but no, Taye and I did nothing together but sleep in the same room. Oh, we did have a couple of meals together," I said, and my mind returned immediately to Avonte.

"What?" Winston asked.

"What?"

"That smile."

"What smile?"

"That cat-that-swallowed-the-rat smile on your face when you talked about dinner. What was that all about?"

"Nothing."

"Nothing huh?" Winston said skeptically. "That look says it was much more than nothing."

"Okay. I did meet somebody while I was there. She was beautiful, vibrant, intelligent, and sexy as hell."

"Did you fuck her?" Winston asked with a horrified look on his face.

"No, no. Nothing like that. We just talked, flirted a little, but that was it."

"Well, that's good to know," Winston said, and breathed a sigh of relief. "Taye's a good woman—too good a woman for you to be cheating on her. I know you guys are having some problems, but cheating is never the answer."

"I know that, Winston. Come on, I love my wife, and I wouldn't do anything to hurt her." I looked at Winston. I knew that Winston liked Taye, but wondered where all this was coming from.

"So what's her name?"

"Who?"

"The woman."

"Frances," I lied, and hoped Winston wouldn't pick up on it. "Frances Nichols."

"Does she live around here?"

"Nope. She's from Los Angeles."

"LA huh? I hear LA women are freaky as hell."

"Yeah, I heard that about them, too. But she lives three thousand miles away. So you can rest assured that I won't be seeing her again."

Winston got up and looked at me. "Good."

As soon as he was gone, I went in the trashcan and took out Avonte's number. I smoothed it out and put it in my desk drawer.

At the end of a very long day, I turned out the lights in my office and made my way home to Rockland County. On the way, I tried to put thoughts of Avonte out of my mind.

The attempt was unsuccessful.

Vivid images of her continued to dominate me. In my mind's eye, I could see images of me making love to Avonte.

I'm sitting quietly on the bed as Avonte walked slowly toward me with her hands behind her back. Then she stopped to allow the sexy red dress she was wearing to drop to the floor. Damn she was so fuckin' fine. Avonte continued coming toward me. Her eyes were ablaze with the passion she was about to share with me. Once she was standing in front of me, Avonte said, "Stand up."

I quickly stood up.

"Take off your clothes," she commanded.

I quickly began to loosen my tie and unbutton my shirt at the same time. "No!" Avonte said.

I stopped.

"Do it slowly. I like to watch."

I smiled at her and did as she asked, slowly and methodically removing each article of my clothing for Avonte's entertainment. Once I was naked, Avonte stepped to me and pressed her naked body against mine. I felt the heat of her body and she felt mine, and we kissed a long and passionate kiss, without using our hands. Our tongues glided effortlessly over each other's, until we stopped for air.

Avonte laid down on the bed, and I ran my hand across her breasts, and then teased them with my tongue, sliding it slowly around her beautiful nipples. Once again, we enjoyed the taste of each other's tongues darting playfully in and out of our mouths. Avonte smiled and touched my face, and then she curled up in the fetal position. I ran my hand over her shoulder and down her arm. Her skin was so soft.

Avonte began to move in response. She rolled into my arms

and kissed my lips. I tasted her tongue as it glided slowly and smoothly over mine. I broke our embrace and spread her legs. I kissed her inner thighs, and then tasted the wetness between them. Avonte held my head in place as my tongue slithered along her lips, making circles around her clit. Her grip grew tighter, her stomach muscles locked, and her head drifted back in quiet ecstasy.

I watched Avonte gliding her hands across my skin to my now throbbing erection. Avonte repositioned herself and straddled my body, as I looked on with great anticipation. She lowered herself onto me. While Avonte took my erection into the wetness between her thighs, I stared into her eyes. They were so intense, so filled with passion that I couldn't look away. Avonte moved her body agonizingly slow, until her body began to tremble.

Avonte rolled off me, and I watched as she crawled around on the bed. I crawled over beside her and ran my hands along her back, around her perfect ass, then squeezed her firm thighs. Avonte spread her legs, and I fingered her clit and played with her lips. I got up on my knees and entered her from behind. Her pussy was tight, yet so very soft, so very wet. I felt her ass pounding against me, felt the muscles inside her tighten around me. The fantasy ended when I pulled into my driveway, into the garage, and turned off my engine.

The house was in darkness when I went inside. Taye's car was in the garage, so I knew she was there. "Taye," I called to her, but got no response. "Taye!" Still, I got no answer.

I wandered around the house turning on lights and looking in each room for her, until I reached our bedroom. I turned on the light and there on the bed, fully clothed, lay Taye. "Hi, baby."

Taye slowly opened her eyes. "Hello," she said.

"You okay?"

"I'm fine."

"You have a good day at work?"

"It was fine."

"Can I get you anything?" I asked.

"No. I told you I'm fine," Taye said, and rolled into the fetal position. "Could you turnoff the light, please?"

I shook my head. "Sure, baby. If you need anything, just let me know," I said, as I turned off the light and closed the door.

I went back downstairs and into the den. I walked over to the bar and grabbed the bottle of Barcardi, and a glass off the shelf. When the glass was full, I drank it down and poured another. I took off my jacket and loosened my tie, before sitting down. I picked up the remote and turned on the CD player. The re-mastered version of the Miles Davis classic *Kind of Blue,* eased gently out of the speakers. The name of the song was "So What", and that was exactly how I felt. And for that, I felt guilty.

I thought back to the first conversation I had with Dr. Larrieux, as she tried to explain to me what Taye was experiencing. "Depression is a serious medical illness, Devin. It's not just something that Taye has made up in her head. It's more than just feeling down in the dumps or blue for a few days. It's feeling down and low and hopeless for weeks at a time."

"I understand," I said. But at the time, I really didn't grasp the magnitude of her condition.

"Taye's type of depression is called bipolar disorder, or manic-depressive illness. It's characterized by cycling mood changes: severe highs or mania, and lows or depression. Sometimes the mood switches are dramatic and rapid, but most often they are gradual. When in the depressed cycle, an individual can have any or all of the symptoms of a depressive disorder."

"And what are those?"

"Persistent sad, anxious, or empty moods," Dr. Larrieux said. "Feelings of hopelessness or pessimism. She could experience feelings of guilt, worthlessness, and or helplessness. It can range from loss of interest or pleasure in hobbies and activities that were once enjoyed, including sex."

"Yeah, she's definitely got that one."

"She could experience decreased energy or fatigue. She may have difficulty concentrating or remembering, or just making simple decisions."

"Okay, Dr. Larrieux, what's the plan?"

"There are a variety of antidepressant medications and psychotherapies that can be used to treat depressive disorders. We are going to start with a combined treatment and medication. My hope is that Taye will gain relatively quick symptom relief, and psychotherapy will help her learn more effective ways to deal with life's problems, including depression."

"What can I do to help?"

"The most important thing you can do is to offer Taye emotional support. This involves understanding, patience, affection, and encouragement. Invite her for walks, outings, go to the movies and other activities. Encourage Taye to participate in some activities that once gave her pleasure, but do not push her to undertake too much too soon. What she needs is diversion and company, but too many demands can increase feelings of failure."

I tried to do everything that Dr. Larrieux suggested. At first it seemed that Taye was responding well to the treatment, but now it seems like she's slipping. Maybe it was too soon for something as big as a trip to Puerto Rico. But then I thought about what the doctor said about the changes sometimes being gradual. As I looked back over the past few weeks, that's exactly what had been happening.

Although at the time I didn't really understand what she was going through, after dealing with it for so long, I felt like I could write a book on the subject–*How to Live With Your Manic-depressive Wife*. "A guaranteed bestseller, for sure," I said, and raised my glass.

After another evening alone drinking and listening to music, I turned off the stereo and went upstairs to bed. Taye was already asleep–with her customary bottle of sleeping pills and half-empty glass of water by her side.

I pulled back the covers and got in bed. I looked at Taye. "My beautiful baby," I said, and touched her face. "Why do you insist on sleeping in sexy lingerie?" I turned off the lights and wondered how long could I keep this up?

Chapter Seven

Avonte

It was late Friday afternoon when my flight arrived at JFK. After Devin left that Sunday, I checked out of the Marriott and caught a charter flight to Isla de Vieques—an island about ten miles to the east of the Puerto Rican mainland. After a weekend of drinking by the pool and hanging out with Devin, I wanted to go someplace quiet to relax. I checked into Martineau Bay Resort & Spa—a plantation-style resort, overlooking the Atlantic Ocean that billed itself as the ultimate island sanctuary. It did give me a chance to really relax and think.

I spent some time thinking about Devin, and patted myself on the back for not sleeping with him, even though I wanted to so very badly. In the back of my mind, I still wanted my marriage, and sleeping with Devin would not be the way to accomplish that. I had made it a point not to discuss any real details about myself. I didn't tell him about the problems Tyrone and I were having, and nothing at all about the fact that I had money. I wouldn't want to think that Devin was interested in me because he thought he was pushing up on money. The fact that he wanted my body was what my ego needed.

I spent the rest of the week there. I hadn't come to any real conclusions, but I was ready to come home. After collecting my luggage, I had a car service take me home. Tyrone and I lived in a house on Windward Road in Glen Cove. It was a traditional townhouse that sat atop a bluff, overlooking the Long Island Sound. I decorated that house and redesigned it, when you get down to it. It was a beautiful house with vaulted ceilings and five bedrooms. I picked out the marble in the house, took months deciding on the granite and wood floors that ran throughout the propriety, as well as those lovely French doors that led to my deck and all those incredible sunsets over Manhattan. As we drove, I wondered just how long I would call it home.

I had the driver drop my bags at the door and tipped him. Once he was gone, I kicked off my shoes and headed straight for my deck. It was unseasonably warm for that time of year in New York, and I thought I'd relax and unwind out there after my flight.

When I opened the French doors and walked out on the deck, what I saw made me stop dead in my tracks. There she was–with her long, blonde hair–with her ass sitting in my chair. *He got his fuckin' nerve bringing his new bitch to my house!* "Umm, excuse me."

Her neck snapped around and she looked at me, and then she smiled. "Oh, I'm sorry. You startled me. You must be Carmen–" she started, but I cut her ass off quick. "No. That's the maid. Who the fuck are you?" I asked, and started walking up on her.

She jumped up from my chair and started backing away from me. "I don't know who you are, but I think you should leave before I call the police."

"The police?" She's gonna call the police on me in my own house. "Go ahead and call them."

"Look," she said, and continued to back away. "If you want money, my purse is inside. You can have it all. Please, just don't hurt me."

When she ran out of deck to back up on, I had her cornered. I slapped her in the face because I knew I wouldn't get another chance, and watched it turn red. "Go ahead and call the police. I'll be upstairs," I told Blondie and went inside.

As I walked through the house, she came back inside, and I could hear her frantic-ass trying to call Tyrone. "Answer the phone, damn it!"

I knew that she was wasting her time. Tyrone had a bad habit of not answering his phone when he was busy, and not checking his messages. His secretary does that for him, and gives him the messages that are important. "Get used to it, sweetie," I said as I walked up the steps.

Since this is such a nice neighborhood, the police were there is less than five minutes. I listened by the door as she explained to the police that some black woman broke into her *boyfriend's* house, and assaulted her.

"Is she still in the house, ma'am?" the officer asked.

"She's upstairs. Probably stealing the jewelry."

"How can I steal my own jewelry, dumb bitch?" I said out loud, and waited for the cops to come upstairs. After I showed them my driver's license listing the house as my address, the officers, realizing the delicate situation they had stumbled into, apologized and went back downstairs to break the news to Blondie.

"His wife?" I heard her say. "That's his wife?"

"Yes ma'am. So I'm afraid you're going to have to leave."

It was hours later when Tyrone finally got to the house. I could no longer call it a home. He had done everything he could to make that clear to me.

My bags were packed and in the car by then, and I was sitting in the living room. All that remained was for me to get some things off my chest, and get out of there. I felt embarrassed and humiliated by the fact that he would bring her to what was once our house.

"Barb," I heard him yell when he came through the door. "I got something for you, baby. Barb, where are you, baby?"

"Not Barb."

"Oh, shit," Tyrone said softly, and came slowly into the living room. "Hello, Avonte. When did you get back?"

"A couple of hours ago. I got here just in time to catch a burglar."

"A burglar?"

"Yes, but the police came and put her out."

When I said *her*, Tyrone sat down in the chair across from me. "Her?"

"Yeah, her," I said, and threw my drink at him. "How could you do that to us, Tyrone?"

"What did I do?"

"Don't play stupid with me, Tyrone, it doesn't suit you. Barb!" I yelled, wishing I had something else to throw at him. "You had your concubine in our house! I was only gone a week, Tyrone. How could you just move another woman in here?"

"I didn't move her in, Avonte. Be reasonable."

I bolted up from the couch. "Be reasonable? Did you fuck her in our bed?" I asked, looking for something to throw. There was a lamp nearby, so I grabbed it and threw it. That got his attention as he jumped out of his seat.

"You got to believe me, Avonte. I didn't move her in. I had a meeting to go to, so I left her here. I didn't think I'd be gone this long, and I definitely wasn't expecting you," Tyrone said, moving around the room as I looked for more stuff to throw.

"So, you brought that bitch over here? Did you fuck her in our house?"

"No."

"Don't lie to me. Do you think I'm some kind of fool?" I threw a vase at him. "You been fucking the bitch all this time, but now you want me to believe that you didn't say, 'Come on, Barbie; let's fuck in your new house?" I picked up a big glass ashtray and threw it at him. That one almost hit him.

"It didn't happen!"

"It doesn't matter!" I shouted back, and threw another lamp at him. "The fact that you brought her here, to our house, proves that you don't have any respect for me. You never have."

"That's not true."

"Yes, it is!" The tears were streaming down my face, and my heart felt like it was going to break out of my chest. I stopped moving, closed my eyes, and tried to calm down. "Why did she think I was the maid?"

"What?" Tyrone asked.

"When I got here, she thought I was Carmen. What's the matter? You didn't tell her that your wife is black?"

"What are you talking about?"

"When I got here, Miss Thing was propped up in my chair on the deck. When I came in, she thought I was the maid instead of your wife. The fucking cops had to tell her I was your wife, and she sounded pretty surprised."

I ran out of the house and heard Tyrone calling my name. I got in the car and left him standing on the lawn screaming, "Avonte!" And I wondered why I was suddenly so important to him.

I checked into the first hotel I got to, and resolved for myself that it was over. I would go see our lawyer in the morning to see where I stood financially, and go from there.

Chapter Eight

Devin

It was another one of those nights; burning the midnight oil, trying to get a project ready to present in the morning. Things had moved along a lot faster than usual for a change, so I sent just about everybody home except Sandra and Eileen, another woman who worked in the office. By one o'clock, Eileen was done with her portion and was more than ready to go home.

"So, Devin, you gonna send me home or what?" Eileen said, standing up gathering her things together.

"Yeah, Eileen, you can jet. And thanks for staying," I said, looking over her work. "Looks good–real good. Maybe you should come in at five in the evening and work until one in the morning every day. You do better work at night."

"You sound like a fool. This is not the kind of night work I like doing. If you dig what I mean," Eileen said, heading for the door. "Sandra, you about done? You want me to wait for you?"

"No, girl. You go ahead on," Sandra said.

"Okay. Now you two kids play nice together. Don't fight."

Sandra and I both laughed. "Don't worry, mom. I promise I'll be good. You won't have to come back and whip us," Sandra said.

"We're just about done here anyway," I said to Eileen, watching her walk toward the door.

The door closed and I got back to work, reviewing the work we had spent the night doing. It was good—damn good, if I do say so myself. The client should be pleased with it. I looked at the clock, thinking I should be done by two. There really wasn't any reason for Sandra to stay, but she always stayed with me until the job was done.

I looked up and noticed that Sandra was standing in the doorway. I wondered how long she'd been standing there. I gave her my very best, genuine, fake smile. "Hi, Sandra," I said, rustling through some papers on my desk, trying to present the impression that I was working, and not fantasizing about having sex with Avonte. "Give me I few more minutes, and we'll be ready to go."

"You know something, Devin . . ." Sandra walked slowly into the office, kind of lifelessly.

She plopped down in the chair and exhaled very deeply. I looked at her eyes. She didn't look tired. But it was almost as though she was dragging herself. Which was out of character for her; Sandra never got tired. I'd seen her go two days in this office without sleep. By the end of the second day, all of us were done, but not Sandra. She was trying to lead us in a sing-a-long of "We Are the World".

". . . I envy you," she said, fanning herself with the report she'd spent all night working on.

"What do you envy about me?"

"You and Taye. Taye really."

"Why's that, Sandra?"

"You two seem so happy together. I mean, you guys just took a romantic trip to Puerto Rico."

I smiled, thinking, *If you only knew the truth of how our relationship was going, you wouldn't say that.* "I love my baby. She's the best thing that ever happened to me," I lied.

"Me and Ike don't do anything together."

"Y'all don't watch television together?"

"When we watch TV, yeah, we're in the same room, but we're not together. He sits in his chair, I sit on the couch, and that's that. It's like we're strangers sometimes."

"You don't think he's fooling around on you, do you?"

"No. Well, at least I don't think so. I mean, when would he have time? I could set a clock by him. He leaves the house the same time every morning, gets home the same time every night. He never goes anywhere. He doesn't have anybody he hangs out with. No one ever calls him, except his family from Texas. I try to get him to go out after work with the guys he works with, but he won't go."

"Y'all don't go anywhere together? Have a drink, catch a flick, nothing? Go to a restaurant; nothing like that?"

"If I don't cook, we don't eat."

"Damn, that's whack."

"Fucked up is what it is," Sandra said, slumping lower in her chair.

I never knew it was like that. I felt bad for her. Sandra was one of the nicest people I knew. Everybody liked her. She was always so alive and friendly. I never would have thought that she was that unhappy. Or was she? "How does that make you feel?" I asked like a psychologist.

"You want me to go lay down on the couch?" Sandra said, as she started to get up.

"Sit down, girl; it ain't that type a party."

"I was about to say . . . since you're trying to psychoanalyze me." We both laughed. Then Sandra got up and walked toward the window. "I tried talking to him about it. But he doesn't think there's anything wrong. He says, 'It ain't like we argue.' And he's right. We don't argue. But sometimes I wish we did. Maybe then he'd show me some passion."

"Hey," I said, pointing a cautioning finger. "Be careful what you wish for."

"You're right. I sure don't wanna go there. But a little emotion would be nice. A little emotion directed at me would be better. Just a little bit of passion, maybe. What am I saying?—A whole lot of passion. I don't think that's a whole lot for a wife to ask of her husband."

"No, it's not," I agreed, thinking that it wouldn't be a whole lot for a husband to ask of his wife.

"See, passion ain't no problem for y'all, is it?"

"Nope. I think we got that part covered," I lied again. But I was thinking about lying on my back and opening my eyes to the site of Avonte riding me.

"So when you get home, you're gonna wake Taye up and go for it. Ain't you?"

"Yes," I lied again, and wondered why I was keeping up this front.

There would be nothing going on in our bedroom that night, or any other night. But it wasn't always like that. I remembered when we first got together. It was like we felt each other sometimes. One minute we'll be talking and we'll just look at each other. The next thing you know, we're naked and into it. And it didn't matter where we were or what was going on around us. We'd do it anywhere.

But it wasn't just our sex life. It was much more than that.

We shared everything. We'd talk all the time. We used to talk to each other at least ten times a day, mostly about nothing. I'd think about her and I'd just call, or something would happen to her at work, and she'd just have to tell me all about it.

"I called Ike when you said we had to work late. You know what he said?" Sandra said, snapping me back to reality.

"I'm afraid to ask."

"Did you cook? That's all he had to say. Not what time will you be home? Not I'll miss you. Not I'll wait up for you. Just wanted to know about some fuckin' food. Like it didn't matter whether I was there or not. You're going home to a woman who loves you, and to get fucked. But me, NOT! No; not me. I might as well sleep on the couch. We barely have sex anymore, and when we do—after I beg, I should say—it's so mechanical."

I didn't comment on that one, because at that point, mechanical sex with Taye would be a step up for us.

"Devin, most nights we just go to sleep. No touching, no kissin', just sleep. And when he does give me what I call 'a mercy fuck', it's like he's running a race or something. Like he's in a hurry to get it over with. And when he's done, that's it. No regard whatsoever for me. He doesn't care whether I get mine or not. It's very frustrating."

"Maybe you should try making it more exciting for him. Wear something sexy. Tempt him, tease him; make him want you."

"Been there, done that. Something sexy, huh? If you only knew, Devin." She laughed. "If you only knew. . . ."

I laughed. I didn't know why, but I laughed. "If I only knew what, Sandra?"

She walked back to the chair and sat down. Then, she smiled

at me. "If you only knew what I had on under these jeans and this blouse."

"What?"

"Let's just say its black and lacy."

"Oooh."

"I like wearing lingerie. I got tons of it. Victoria's Secret, Frederick's of Hollywood, all that. I love it."

"Oh, really." I never thought she went for stuff like that. She always seemed so plain; dressed in pants every day. I seemed to remember her having nice legs when I hired her, but that was the last time I saw them. I guess you never really know.

"Does that surprise you? Never mind. I can tell by that look in your eyes. You didn't think I was the sexy lingerie type. Well, I am, big time."

"He doesn't like you in it?"

"He used to. I guess it got old, common. You know what I mean?"

"Try something else."

"What do you have in mind? I've tried everything I can think of."

"Like what?" Now I was curious. Just how far had she gone? Sandra was an attractive woman. A little on the bony side for my personal taste, but attractive. You wouldn't think she'd have to go through no whole group of changes just to get her freak on. But what did I know.

"Tell me something; if you came home, and you found the house lit with candles and a trail of Taye's clothes leading into the bedroom, would you follow it?"

"Yeah; 'cause I'd know that she was waiting for me at the other end of the trail. Why, didn't he?"

"Devin, I'm laying in the bed, butt naked. I got incense burning and soft music playing to set the mood. I hear the door open and close. I spread my legs and I waited, and waited. Next thing I know, the TV is on and I hear that guy yelling, 'Let's get ready to rumble!'"

"Hey, you just picked the wrong night. Men take fight night very seriously."

"I know that. It's a man thing, right?" She smiled a fake smile.

"Right." I smiled back. "Who was fighting?"

"That's what pissed me off. It was some old fight on ESPN Classic. It was that bald guy, umm, Marvin Hagler, and some guy with a bad Jheri curl."

"Hey, I think I might've had to pass, too. That guy with the curl was Tommy 'The Hit Man' Herns. And that was one of the greatest fights in middle-weight history."

"Yeah, yeah, that's exactly what he said. So what? Fight didn't even last long."

"But what there was, was great." I got up and sat down on the couch. "Great fight."

"Anyway, I've tried everything from nasty movies to serving him a candlelit dinner, naked. Nothing about it seems to get him excited. Nothing about me excites him. I'm twenty-nine years old. I need to feel like a woman. I need to feel wanted. And I don't. And I hate it," Sandra said, once again slumping deep in the chair.

"I'm sorry." What else could I say? No one should have to go through life like that. A passionless relationship like the one I had. I knew exactly what it felt like sleeping with Taye every night and not touching her, not kissing her, not feeling her body next to mine. Not being inside her.

I was ready to go. Sandra was starting to depress me. But I

felt like I had to hear her out. I considered Sandra a friend, and she was baring her soul to me. The last thing she needed was for me to seem disinterested, or that I didn't care because I was getting mine. I looked over at Sandra. She looked so sad sitting there straining to rub her neck. I got up and walked behind her chair. I moved her hands out of the way and began to massage her neck. "Damn, girl. You really are tense."

"That's what I been trying to tell you. I'm surprised that I don't have big bumps all over my face."

"Maybe you should buy some toys or something, make it fun."

"I thought about that, don't think I didn't. But I'm just too ashamed to go up in one of those places."

"Why? Everybody in there is there for the same reason: trying to find just the right thing to make it more interesting."

"You ever been to one?"

"Me and Taye go sometimes." At least we used to. "Some of the stuff they got is pretty wild."

"But you do it together. That's what's important. Y'all do it together. Right there, Devin. Yeah, that feels good." She was rocking her head from side to side.

"Maybe you should take him with you. I mean, that will serve two purposes. You'd be doing something together, and then you get to go home and have some fun doing something together."

"A little lower. Between my shoulder blades." Sandra unbuttoned a few buttons on her blouse and pushed it off her shoulders. Under that blouse she was wearing a spaghetti strapped black lace teddy. "Thought I was kidding about the lace, huh? I like the way it feels against my skin. Makes me feel sexy."

I stopped.

"Don't stop. You were just gettin' there."

"Chill out. Who's doing this? You just sit there and relax. Leave the hard work to me. Cool?"

"Cool. Just don't stop. Cool?"

"Cool."

"Cool."

Neither of us said anything for a while. I marveled at how many similarities there were between the way Ike used to treat Sandra, and the way me and Taye were.

"Anyway, Devin, I've tried everything. I just don't know what else to do," Sandra said, as she hunched her shoulders. "It wasn't always like this. When we were in Texas, my God, he was all over me–all the time. In the bed, on the stairs, anywhere. There wasn't a piece of furniture that we hadn't done it on. Surprised me for lunch, and sometimes we'd just go to the motel and get busy for lunch." She laughed. "I remember one night we had planned to go to dinner, and he was supposed to pick me up when I got off work, right? I didn't see him, so I started to get in my car and drive home. I opened the door, and there were a dozen roses on the front seat, and he was hiding in the backseat. He was so attentive. He'd call me four, five times a day. You know what I'm talking 'bout, like you call Taye. Now, hmmph, when the phone rings, I know it's not him."

"Doesn't even sound like the same guy. What happened?"

"I have no clue. After we moved here, things just changed."

"Why'd y'all move here anyway?"

"Opportunity. I wasn't getting anywhere in San Antonio."

"What about Ike?"

"Huh?"

“I didn’t stutter. What about Ike?”

“What do you mean, ‘what about Ike’?”

“I mean, how did he feel about it? How was he doing in San Antonio? I mean, was he all for the move?”

“He wasn’t with it at all at first, but he came around.”

“How did you convince him?”

“I just told him I was going with or without him.” Then she smiled a very satisfied smiled.

“You broke him. Took that man’s spirit, didn’t you?”

“What you talking ’bout, Devin. He’s doin’ better here than he ever has.”

“Doesn’t matter.”

And it didn’t. Not to her. A man gotta at least feel like he’s in control, even if he’s not. I could tell she was thinking about it though. I kept working and tried not to think about it. I closed my eyes and thought about all the times I’d massaged Taye’s shoulders after she’d had a bad day. I worked her shoulders, her neck, her temples, and then worked my way back down to her neck. I put my thumbs in the notches between her neck and shoulders, massaging her upper chest, and for a while, I lost myself in thoughts of Avonte.

I felt her hand touch mine, and she led my hand down. Before I could react, I had a handful of breast. It wasn’t much, but what there was, was all nipple. I squeezed it gently between my thumb and forefinger. She touched my other hand and led it down to the other one.

Sandra started unbuttoning the rest of the buttons on her blouse, and took it off while I continued playing with her nipples. She kicked off her shoes, unbuckled her jeans, and arched her back to come out of them.

I came to her and she threw her arms around my neck, and her tongue down my throat. Sandra undressed me as quickly as she could, and dropped to her knees. She took me into her mouth and sucked until I was hard. Then Sandra pushed me down on the couch and began fucking me like she hadn't had a dick in her in a very long time. I stared into Sandra's eyes the entire time, but my mind was on Avonte. I tried to put the thoughts of her out of my mind, and began to feast on Sandra's nipples. When I began to feel her legs trembling on my thighs, I pushed harder. Sandra bore down on me and increased her pace. I could feel that she was about to come. She reached out and touched my face with both hands, and kissed me.

I closed my eyes and thought about how Taye used to ride me like there was no tomorrow. What the fuck was I doing?

"What the fuck am I doing?" I said out loud this time, as if I had been jerked back to reality.

Sandra got up. "I'm sorry, Devin." She smiled at me like the cat that swallowed the chicken. "I don't know what came over me."

It wasn't what she said. It was the way she said it—like it really didn't bother her at all. The look in her eyes told a different story than the one coming out of her mouth.

"No, it was my fault. I got a little carried away."

"I think we both did," she said, smiling, picking up her clothes, and backing out of my office slowly.

We both laughed about it and agreed it shouldn't have happened, and that it would never happen again. Both of us got our things quietly, and left. On the way home, I thought about what had happened. How I should have never put myself in that position.

I thought about Avonte. The guilt came down on me hard then. I thought about telling Taye everything, but what would that accomplish?

Chapter Nine

Avonte

I went to see our lawyer, Albert Weinstein, that next morning after I left Tyrone's house, he was expecting me, naturally. He said that Tyrone planned to file for divorce, and that it would be a good idea for me to, "Obtain the services of another attorney to see over your affairs."

Then he told me that Tyrone had made provisions for me, and hoped that we could settle this matter amicably.

Ain't that a bitch?

There he was talking about ending my marriage like it was just another business deal. I was about to say something smart, but Weinstein handed me an envelope.

"What's this?"

"A check, my dear. You come see me on or about the first of each month, and I'll have it ready for you. Or, I could have it sent to you via courier once you get established."

I opened the envelope and looked at the check. It was for twenty thousand dollars. I was about to be a bitch and say that it wasn't enough, but then I did the math. That would come to little less than a quarter of a million dollars a year. I put the check in my purse and stood up. "You tell Tyrone that I'm sure we can conclude this matter amicably. I will let you know when I obtain the services of another attorney to see over my affairs."

"I'll be expecting their call," Weinstein said as I left his office.

That same day, I rented an apartment and went shopping for furniture. Once I was settled, I gave Weinstein my new address, and that was that. Every first of the month, a courier arrived with my money. It didn't take me long to get tired of being alone.

I got up, got dressed, and went to a nearby bar. I sat down on the barstool, determined to sex the first good-looking man that approached me. I had never done anything even close to this before, but I was able to rationalize it by convincing myself that I'd never been in a situation like this before.

It didn't take long before one stepped up. I didn't even ask him what his name was, and lied when he asked me mine. Before too long, we were leaving the bar and on our way to get a room.

I was on a mission, and nothing was going to get in my way. Once we were in the room and I had stripped him down, I began to wonder what this was going to accomplish. The answer was nothing, but I had taken it this far and there was no way to back out now. I used my tongue to make circles around his nipples then quickly flicked it over one.

"You are so fuckin' fine," he said.

I thought to myself, *Whatever. Just fuck me so I can go.* He gripped my thighs with both hands, and pushed my legs open. He used his fingers to hold my lips apart, and slid his tongue inside me. My clit grew harder as he licked me with the tip of his tongue. Pussy eating definitely wasn't his strong suit, so I pushed him back when I couldn't take it anymore. I put a condom on him and straddled him. With my eyes shut, I rode him slowly; grinding my hips until he was deep inside me. At least he didn't have a little dick.

After I got mine, I rolled off of him. I was ready to go. Before I could say anything, he stood, stepped up behind me, and motioned for me to move to the edge of the bed. He bent me over, and then entered me slowly. Then, he grabbed me by the shoulders and thrust himself farther inside. He began to pound furiously. It didn't take long after that before I felt him expand inside me, and then he collapsed on my back.

He was breathing hard and patting himself on the back for the job he thought he had done on me. I didn't have the heart, or care enough to tell him otherwise. I scooped my clothes and went into the bathroom. I showered quickly and got dressed. When I came out, he was lying on the bed, stroking himself. "Ready for round two?" he asked.

"Only in your dreams," I said, and headed for the door. This was a bad idea from the start. What I should have done was call Devin, except for the fact that I didn't have his number. He did tell me where he worked, and now, more than ever, I was determined to find him.

Chapter Ten

Qianna

After I left LA I went back to New York. On the bus ride across country, I slept a lot. But when I wasn't sleeping, I thought about the fact that I had killed two more people. I told myself that both them niggas had it coming. Niggas shouldn't have tried to cheat me, and they definitely shouldn't have put they fuckin' hands on me. That was some shit I wasn't havin'.

But the shit was that I didn't feel bad about the shit at all. I felt good. I felt like I did when I killed that nigga that beat my ass and raped me. Only difference was, this time I wasn't on my way to jail for it. This time, I had enough fuckin' sense to get the fuck outta dodge before the cops got on to me.

The long-ass ride did give me a chance to think about my temper. I knew that I was too fuckin' quick to pull my blade and shove it in a nigga that crossed me. At the time, I had to ask myself what was so wrong about that. Niggas shouldn't have been fuckin' wit' me. I replayed both murders over in my mind, and thought about what I coulda done different.

Nothing.

That was the answer I came up wit'. Bottom line, I have never taken no shit off nobody, and I wasn't about to start. Niggas need to not be fuckin' wit' me, and I won't have to kill them.

I hadn't been back in the city for very long when I started rollin' wit' these two young ballers, Levon and Craig. Them niggas thought that I was so fine, and they were both kind of cute, so I let them share me.

The three of us were sitting on the couch smokin' weed and drinkin, watchin' a movie. Really we was doin' more talkin' and gettin' fucked up then watchin' the movie, but anyway, somehow they got to talkin' about how much they wanted to see me dance for them. "Why don't you get up and show us what you really about." I got up and started shakin' my ass. I unsnapped my jeans and pulled them down a little, so they could see some of my ass. They started hollerin' for me to take it all off. I wiggled out of them jeans and slowly peeled off the throng I was wearin'. "Can you make it slap?" Craig shouted.

"Hell yeah," I shouted back, and made my cheeks slap.

I turned around, kneeled on the couch, bent over and shook my ass. Levon quickly slapped my ass, while Craig ran his hand across my ass and down my thigh. "Damn, you got some thick-ass thighs, Qianna." I held on to the back of the couch and shook my ass a little longer, while they both felt my body.

I got up from couch and took off my blouse and bra, then sat down between them and put one leg over each of their thighs. Levon started feelin' my titties while Craig just stared between my legs, like he had never seen pussy before. Levon started playin' with my clit and squeezin' my titties. Since Craig seemed so fascinated by my fresh Brazilian wax, I guided his bald head to it so he could get a closer look. He kissed one thigh and then the other, then he bit one cheek, and then the other. He stuck his tongue in my ass before he attacked my clit.

Levon kneeled on the couch and unzipped his jeans. I took him in my mouth. After a while, they switched places so I should suck Craig's dick, but Levon didn't seem interested in suckin' no pussy. He pulled me up, bent me over the couch, and pushed himself inside of me. Craig got up and walked behind the couch, and put his dick back in my mouth. I fucked the shit outta them niggas.

After a while, they found out that I was a bitch with enough heart to do what needed to be done. We was all makin' crazy money. I was really after one of 'em's girlfriend, but that's a story for another day.

Anyway, Levon decided that he wanted to put his hands on me, and then had the nerve to talk shit about it. "No, you didn't just slap me?"

The bastard laughed and so did Craig. "Next time, bitch, I'll do more than slap your bitch-ass."

"Next time?" I got my blade out of my purse. "Nigga, there ain't gonna be no next time."

The fool was laughing so hard, high-fivin' wit' his boy, that he didn't even see me comin'.

"See how you like this, bitch?" I swung my blade and cut him on his neck. It didn't hurt him. It was such a small cut, but it was on his jugular vein. He didn't even know he was bleedin' 'til Craig told him.

"Yo, man, you bleedin'. I mean bleedin' bad."

"Where?"

"On your neck. She fucked you up bad." Levon put his hand on his neck, and then looked down at his shirt, which by now was covered wit' his blood.

"What? You want some, too?" I asked Craig when he stepped to me.

"I'll kill you for this, bitch," Levon said, still holding his neck.

"Whatever," I said, and backed out the door.

"Let her go, man. You need to go to the hospital. We'll get her ass later."

Well, they didn't get my ass later, but the cops did. Since I'd cut him on the jugular vein, they charged me with attempted murder. The only reason he survived was 'cause he applied pressure to it right away. He testified that he had pressed so hard, for so long, that the paramedics had to literally pry his hands away. The doctor who treated him testified that he sutured off the jugular vein to control the bleeding, and since it was on the external jugular vein and not the internal, which is much bigger, and the carotid artery and vagus nerve were not damaged, he expected a full recovery. I took a plea and plead guilty to aggravated assault, and got sentenced to five years at Bedford.

On my first day at Bedford, I knew it wouldn't be long before somebody tried me. I was ready for her. In fact, I wanted somebody to try me so I could make my rep, and nobody else would fuck wit' me. It didn't take long.

I had been there for a week, and was walkin' across the yard when I passed by a group of white bitches, and one of them decided she wanted to holla. "That's one fine nigger bitch there."

I turned around and went right at her. She was a lot bigger than me, but I didn't care. "What you say?"

She stepped up. "I said you was one fine nigger bitch."

Before she got the word "bitch" out her mouth good, I was on her ass. It didn't take long before the guards came and pulled me off her.

They sent us both to the hole. The whole time we was on lockdown, this bitch is callin' me out. I mean yellin' at the top of her lungs about how she was gonna kick my ass when we got out the hole. I didn't even bother to answer her, but I knew what I had to do.

On the day the guard came to take me back to population, I had a plan. When I was leavin', the guard told her to get ready 'cause he would be back for her next. After I was checked into my buildin', I went right back out and went to the isolation unit, and waited outside for her to come out.

As soon as she was close enough to me, I rushed her. Before the guard could stop me, I had her on the ground and was poundin' her in the face. When they finally got me off her, her face was bloody, and I was on my way back to the hole.

When I got out the hole this time, they made me talk to the shrink. Her name was Dr. Carol Goodwin. After a couple of sessions wit' her, she told me that I had anger issues. "Let's face it; anger is a fact of life. Our world is filled with violence, hatred, war, and aggression. Psychologically, many theories of human development focus on the infant's struggle with anger and frustration, and the primitive fantasies of aggression, guilt, and reparation that result from these feelings. In essence, we grow up with anger right from the beginning of life."

"So what all that mean to me?"

"That anger is a natural human emotion. It's nature's way of empowering us to ward off our perception of an attack or threat to our well-being."

"I know what you sayin'. Somebody come at me, I just go off."

"The problem is not anger. The problem is the mismanagement

of anger. Mismanaged anger and rage is the major cause of conflict in our relationships with other people. I suggest that you take an anger management class."

"What the fuck is that?"

"The term anger management commonly refers to a system of psychological therapeutic techniques and exercises, by which someone with excessive or uncontrollable anger can control or reduce the triggers, degrees, and effects of an angered emotional state. One technique for controlling anger is finding agreement with another person, rather than conflict. The use of deep breathing and meditation can be used as a means of relaxation. As the issue of anger varies from person to person, the treatments are designed to be personal to the individual."

Since I didn't have shit else to do, I took the class and really got into it. It taught me a lot about myself, and the source of my rage. I learned ways to deal with my anger like, takin' a timeout and counting to ten before reacting, or puttin' some space between me and the person I'm angry with.

"Once you're calm, express your anger. It's healthy to express your frustration in a non-confrontational way," Dr. Goodwin said. "Stewing about it will only make the situation worse."

She told me that I need to think carefully before I say anything. "Then instead of focusing on what made you mad, work with the person who angered you to resolve the issue."

"I don't know about that one, Doc. You run up on a mad mutha fucka, they ain't tryin' to hear, let's work it out."

"I can understand how that might be the case, but you could use 'I' statements when describing the problem. This will help you to avoid criticizing or placing blame, which can make the other person angry or resentful, and increase the tension between you."

"Like what?"

"For instance, say, 'I am upset you didn't help with the housework this evening,' instead of, 'You should have helped with the housework'."

At first, I didn't think none of that shit was gonna work, but Doc told me to at least try some of the techniques we talked about, and I would see that they work. She said that I shouldn't hold grudges. Try to use humor to release tensions. "Lightening up can help diffuse tension," Doc said. "Don't be sarcastic though."

I laughed. "Why not?"

"It can hurt people's feelings and make things worse. And I strongly recommend that you practice relaxation skills. Learning skills to relax can also help control your temper. Practice deep-breathing exercises, or repeat a calming word or phrase to yourself, like 'Take it easy, Qianna'."

I tried some of the shit she told me, and it worked. Now I'm not gonna say that I was an ideal inmate after that. I still got into my share of shit, and got wrote up for shit almost daily. But I did manage to stay out the hole the rest of the time I was there. I did all of my time, and now, I'm out. And I swore to myself that I was never goin' back to jail ever again. This time, it's gonna be different.

Chapter Eleven

Devin

Taye was up early. It was unusual, given the recent progression of her depression, for her to be up at five-thirty in the morning. But I took it as an opportunity to talk, and hopefully, clear the air between us. We'd been going at it lately, so I braced myself for an argument, but I still went to her with an open heart; and thoughts of Avonte on the backburner.

She was sitting at the dining room table drinking coffee when I found her.

"Mind if I join you?" I asked, and pulled a mug from the cabinet. She shrugged her shoulders. "Taye, we need to talk."

"I really don't feel like it, Devin."

"I know, honey, but we need to."

"So, talk then."

"Taye, you know I love you."

"Is this where you tell me that you're leaving me?"

"Don't be ridiculous or sarcastic. I didn't come to you to argue."

"So, what exactly do you want?" She looked at me with no emotion.

"I want us to be like we used to be. We used to love to be around each other. We used to look forward to touching each other after a long day of tedious work. We used to make love."

"Is that what this about? I told you that you can take it whenever you want."

"Take it? I don't want to take it. I want you to want to make love to me. Don't you want to feel the heat and passion that I have for you, Taye?" I knelt down in front of her. "Don't you want me to love you like you deserve to be loved? We can get through all of these hard times. Remember for better or for worse?"

Taye laughed lethargically.

"For better or for worse; and can it get any worse than it is right now?" I said softy, but Taye still heard me.

"What is that supposed to mean?" she asked.

"I mean, can you think of anything worse than what we have going on right now?"

She got up and went into the kitchen to get another cup of coffee.

"Yes," Taye said, and turned around abruptly.

I was afraid to ask what would be worse. "Living without you, Taye. I swear, you mean everything to me. I need to be desired by you as much as you are by me. That's what husbands and wives do."

"Now we're back to the sex thing. I tell you, you're so predictable, Devin." That offended me, and I wondered if she could predict, that since the day I met her, I wanted to lay with her, make love to her, kiss her lips—both of them, and taste her juices.

"Taye, any other man would leave you."

"Is that what you want to do, Devin? Leave?"

"No. That's why I'm talking to you. I've been trying to talk to you and be here for you, but you keep shutting me out. I'm human, Taye. Damn it!"

"And so am I. But right now, I can't. I have so much healing to do, and you need to give me that time and space to do so."

"And what am I supposed to do in the meantime?"

"Well, you said it, for better or for worse. Be my husband if you love me so much." She went back to the dining room table and took a seat.

"I do love you, baby," I said, as I eased over to her. I took the coffee mug from her hands and began to massage her shoulders. That made her very uncomfortable.

"Don't, Devin." She pushed my hand off her.

Avonte wouldn't tell me no, I thought, and tried to touch her again.

"Don't! I don't want you to touch me!" She screamed, and threw the coffee mug against the wall.

"Taye, have you lost your mind?"

"I asked you not to touch me," she said, as she began to cry hysterically.

"Don't worry. I won't anymore." I left the dining room area and went to get dressed for work.

The rest of the week was like living alone. Taye was in a trance because of her depression. She and I would pass each other like strangers in our own home. I started staying late at the office so that I didn't have to go home and see Taye. I started sleeping on the couch, and while I was alone at night, Avonte danced through my mind, and was the only thing that made my days bearable.

There were so many times I thought of calling her. But every time I picked up the phone and began dialing the number, I'd hang up, and never make the call. My mind was twisted with the love I had for my wife, and the lust I had for Avonte.

How could Avonte have me out there like that? Before Avonte, Taye was the only woman that challenged me sexually and mentally.

But since I met Avonte, it's like she tapped into my mind, and programmed me to think only of her. The more Taye pushed me away, the more I knew I had to have Avonte.

"Thank God it's Friday," I said quietly, as I came out of yet another meeting. It had been a rough week, but I got through it without too much grief and aggravation at the office.

However, on the home front, Taye was slipping deeper and deeper into depression. There were no longer any manic moments, and Dr. Larrieux was considering other therapy alternatives. I was at my wits end, and had begun searching for a new therapist. The entire experience had left me feeling drained.

When I got back to my office, my phone was ringing. "This is Devin James," I said.

"What are you doing?"

"Excuse me," I said, not catching the voice.

"I said what are you doing?"

"Avonte?" I asked, wondering how she got my number, but overjoyed that she had it.

"Yes," Avonte said.

Suddenly I no longer felt drained. I could feel her energy come through the phone, and I fed into it immediately. "How have you been?"

"I'm fine. How come you haven't called me?"

"I lost your number," I lied quickly.

"Yeah, right. You probably balled up my note and threw it away."

"No, I didn't. In fact, I was looking at your number one day and was about to call you, when one of my colleagues came into my office to discuss a case. I haven't been able to find it since then," I said, as close to the truth as I could get on short notice.

"So how have you been?" Avonte asked, seemingly satisfied with my answer.

"I've been all right."

"That's good.

"What about you, Avonte? How have you been doing?"

"I'm good today, but the last few days have been a little rough."

"Anything I can do to help?"

"Just hearing your voice is helping, believe me." Then Avonte dropped her voice an octave. "I wanna see you, Devin James."

"I'd like to see you, too. Avonte, would you mind holding on for a minute?"

"Sure."

I put Avonte on hold and got up from my desk. I went to my office door, then closed and locked it, before returning to the phone.

"Thanks for holding, Avonte."

"Not a problem. So, when am I going to see you?"

"What are you doing this evening?"

"Seeing you," Avonte replied definitely.

"Why don't we meet someplace for dinner."

"That's fine. Where and when?"

"Do you mind coming into the city?"

"Not really."

"Are you familiar with the South Street Seaport?"

"Yes. I've been there a few times," Avonte said.

"There's a restaurant there called Sequoia."

"I know the place. I've eaten there before. The food is good. What time?"

"Is seven good for you?" I asked.

"That's perfect, Devin. That will give me some time to get

some things done around here."

"So, I'll see you at seven then?"

"It's a date," Avonte said quickly; and abruptly hung up the phone.

I sat holding the phone in my hand for a second or two longer, before returning it to its cradle. I glanced over at the clock. It was almost two o'clock. I picked up the phone, dialed Taye at work, and told her that I was having dinner with a client, and wouldn't be home until late in the evening. "No later than midnight, I'd think," I said. I figured I'd meet Avonte at seven. Have dinner, drinks, and little conversation, add another hour in case the service is bad or the conversation is good, and on the way home by eleven.

Taye's response was, "Fine." It was getting to be her standard response to anything.

For the remainder of the afternoon, I was riding a wave of adrenaline. Not even Winston's constant questions about why I seemed so "damned bubbly", could break me out of it. Almost from the first moment I saw her, I felt an intense physical attraction to her. From the start, Avonte was all up in my face, giving me a strong vibe that she wanted me.

Whenever my mind wasn't occupied, it always seemed to eventually drift to thoughts of Avonte. It would always go the same way—me with my clothes off, longing to be inside her. I imagined myself doing it to her slow with the lights low, licking her plump nipples then fuckin' her doggie-style.

I thought about Taye. I loved her so much and wished that she would get better, but I needed sex. I needed to feel the warmth of a woman's flesh against mine.

At seven o'clock sharp, I stood waiting on Pier 17 at the South

Street Seaport. Thinking that it would be rude if I went inside and waited for her to arrive at the bar, I decided to wait outside. It was a particularly cold night, so I hoped that Avonte wouldn't be too late.

By seven thirty, I decided that waiting outside was no longer an option, and went inside. Taking a seat at the bar so I could see the door, I waited. My hands and face were cold, so I shot my first glass of Barcardi trying to get warm.

It was a little after eight when Avonte finally came through the door. As soon as she saw me, Avonte smiled that beautiful smile of hers, and came to me. I stood up to greet her and tried to give her a platonic hug, and keep a polite distance between us, but Avonte would have none of that. She put her body into it and topped it off with a kiss on the lips.

"Sorry I'm so late. Traffic coming through the Midtown Tunnel was murder."

"You made it, and that's the important thing."

"I would have called to let you know I was going to be late, but you didn't give me your cell phone number." She took off her coat to reveal a one-piece black jumper, accented with a diamond studded waist belt.

"You look incredible tonight, Avonte."

"Thank you, Devin," Avonte flirted in that voice that was driving me insane. "You look very nice in a suit."

Once we were seated, a waiter came and handed us menus. As he told us about the day's specials, Avonte said, "Oysters. Do you like oysters?"

"I love oysters."

"Good," Avonte said, turning her attention to the waiter. "We'll start out with a dozen of your East and West Coast oysters. And bring me a double shot of Kettle One." She sent the waiter on his way.

"So, Avonte, other than the oysters, do you see anything else you like?"

"Well, the pan-fried crab cake with roasted potatoes, seasonal vegetables, and tartar sauce sounds tasty. But, I think I'm going to have the fried sea scallops with whipped potatoes and chive oil. What about you?"

"I was looking at the roasted Maine lobster, but that's too much trouble, so I'm gonna try the linguine with fresh clams."

Over dinner, we had the usual amount of polite dinner conversation. I talked about my life as tax attorney.

"Boring," Avonte mused. "But you didn't invite me to dinner to talk about my taxes."

"Really," I laughed a little. "Why did I invite you then, Ms. Avonte?"

"You invited me here because you want me."

I didn't answer right away, but since that is why I invited her there, I went on and admitted it. "You're right, I do want you."

"I usually am about these things." Avonte smiled.

"So when can we get together?" I asked as I discreetly glanced at my watch.

"What about now?"

I glanced at my watch again. It was little before ten; so much for on the way home by 11. "Now is good," I said, and signaled for the waiter.

Chapter Twelve

Avonte

Now that the check had been paid and the waiter was tipped handsomely, Devin and I left the restaurant and stepped out into the cold night air.

"Where to?" I asked.

"I know a place not far from here."

"Where is that?"

"A hotel called Club Quarters. It's on Williams Street. It's only a couple of blocks from here. We can walk, if you like."

"You know, Devin, if it's all the same to you, why don't we just catch a cab," I suggested. "I know walking would be more, you know, romantic, but it's cold. And I want you now."

Devin stepped to the curb. "Taxi!" he yelled.

A short time later, we were walking in the hotel lobby of Club Quarters. "I take it you come here often?"

"Yes. My office is near here, so we put up clients here when they're in town. And anytime somebody works late and doesn't want to go home, this is where we stay."

"Convenient."

"Yeah, we even get a corporate discount."

The desk clerk handed Devin the card key, and we proceeded to the elevator. When the door was closed, Devin inserted the key in the slot and pressed the button for our floor. I immediately stepped to him. I put my arms around his neck and kissed him.

When the elevator stopped on our floor, the door opened and closed again. We continued kissing. When the elevator opened again, we were back in the lobby. We looked at each other and smiled, and quickly turned to laugher.

"Maybe we should try it again," I suggested, "without the kissing part this time."

"You think?" Devin said, laughing as he put the card key in again.

"I promise to behave myself this time, but I can't say for how long."

"Is that a threat or a promise?"

"Believe me, it's both."

I kept my word and stood on the opposite side of the elevator. When it reached our floor, we got off and started down the hall. "Tell me, when we get to the room, are we going to have one of those scenes where we start ripping each other's clothes off like two mad dogs in heat?" Devin asked.

"That is so done," I answered, and took hold of Devin's hand. "So, I tell you what, I'll undress you, and then you can undress me. How does that sound?"

"Sounds like a real plan to me," Devin said as he unlocked the door and we went in.

"I know what I just said, but . . ." I said, taking off my coat and stepping out of my shoes.

"But what?"

"I have this overpowering urge to start ripping your clothes off, and fuckin' the shit out of you like a mad dog in heat."

Devin took off his coat and jacket. "Do you?"

"Yes, but unzip me first."

I turned around and Devin did as I asked, and then he took his time undressing me. He did it so slowly that I could tell he wanted to make every second of this last.

I did too.

Before that last night in San Juan, it had been so long since I'd felt a man's body against mine.

"Thank you. I've been dying to get out of that jumper all night," I said, and placed it neatly on the chair. Then I turned around and walked toward Devin, and began to undress him. Before I got his shirt off, Devin drew me to him and kissed me. Devin's eyes were on fire. I could tell from that look and how hard he was, just how much he wanted me. I put my arms around his neck and pressed my body against his. The heat from my body made him grow harder as we kissed passionately. Our tongues glided effortlessly in and out of each other's mouths, just as I'd imagined so many times. We explored each other's bodies with our hands until I abruptly stopped.

"What's wrong?"

"Nothing," I smiled, and playfully pushed Devin down on the bed. Then I sat beside him and looked at his erection, which was standing as straight as the Washington Monument. "Damn, you got a big dick," I whispered. "And I love a big dick."

I clasped my fingers together and placed them around his throbbing dick. Slowly, but ever so firmly, I moved my hands up and down. I began to fondle his balls with one hand and stoked him with the other. I licked my lips, and I felt his dick swelling in my hand. His balls were getting fat too, so I squeezed them lightly, let go his of dick, and lowered my head to him.

Devin propped a pillow behind his head and watched me as my tongue slid up and down his dick. With my thumb and forefinger, I squeezed the bottom of its shaft, causing his head to swell. I ran circles around his head with my tongue. Devin tried to reach for me, but I stopped what I was doing and moved his hand away.

I ran my tongue over my lips and gently kissed his head. I slid my moistened lips down on him. Up and down, deeper and deeper, slowly, until I had taken almost all of him in my mouth.

I could tell by the look on his face that Devin was in ecstasy.

His body became tense and rigid, and I felt him begin to expand inside my mouth, as I licked and sucked him. I knew he was getting ready to come, so I stopped. I squeezed his dick in my hand and felt it twitching. "I'm not ready for you to come yet," I said, lying next to him, spreading my legs. "Come here."

Devin started at my ankles and kissed his way up my inner thighs, until he found the wetness between them. He pulled back the foreskin around my clit and held it, while he licked his finger and began to gently massage it. Devin looked into my eyes. Our eyes locked and I moaned.

His tongue slithered along my lips, and then made tight circles around my clit, while he moved his finger in and out of my dripping wet pussy. "That feels so good."

My stomach muscles locked, my thighs began to tremble, and my toes curled against the sheets. My mouth and eyes opened wide, and I grabbed Devin's head. "Yes, baby, yes!" I screamed, and my head drifted back in ecstasy.

I rolled away from Devin, smiling, shaking, and breathing

hard. He allowed me a second or two to catch my breath before he came toward me. Devin lay beside me and gently touched my face. He kissed my lips and began to roll to me.

I put my hands on his shoulders, pushed Devin on his back, and rolled on top of him. Without a word, I raised myself over his body, grabbed his dick, and slowly lowered myself onto him.

The feeling of finally having Devin inside me after imagining and wanting him as intensely as I had, for so long, was indescribable. Devin laid on his back in awe, as I moved my body up and down on him, grinding my hips into him with each stroke. He slid his hands from my shoulders, down my back, and then gripped my ass. I leaned forward and kissed Devin, while I continued my ride. He began to push back furiously. I stepped my pace up a notch.

"You're gonna make me come again!" I yelled, and sat straight up on him. Once again, my head drifted back and my mouth opened wide. Devin gently twisted my nipples. "Fuck me, Devin!" I screamed.

Devin smiled.

I rolled off him, but immediately got up on my knees. "Come on," I demanded, and Devin stood up and fell in behind me. He entered me slowly, easing in inch by inch. My pussy was so wet and his dick was so hard. Devin began to pump it to me. "Don't tease me. I wanna feel all of you in me."

Devin ignored my demand and continued his slow, almost methodical pace, until he was deep inside me. He grinded his hips into me and tapped my ass lightly. He increased his pace. "Yeah, that's it. Fuck me."

I began to push back, and slid my hand between my legs and massaged my clit. I could tell by the look on his face that Devin felt my pussy tightening around his dick. He reached for my shoulders and pounded himself into me. I came again. I couldn't remember ever coming so many times so fast, not even with Tyrone. Devin continued, and I felt myself about to come again. I forced myself to pull away from him. I rolled on my back and looked at Devin standing over me, still rock hard.

Since my legs were still open wide, Devin took that as an invitation to suck my pussy again. He literally dove between my thighs and went for it. I wasn't about to stop him from doing anything he wanted, within reason of course. It had been so long since I'd had some good loving, and I wanted to get all I could.

I came again.

I pushed his head away from my dripping, and now very sensitive, pussy. I pulled him to me, and he entered me in a single stroke. He placed the weight of his body on his arms, and I arched my back and rotated my hips in perfect unison with him, moving slow, then fast, and then slow again. My body began to quiver. My heartbeat quickened along with our pace, until we screamed together.

Chapter Thirteen

Devin

The sound of the alarm came way too early for me that morning. It was after two when Avonte finally let me close my eyes. It felt like I hadn't been to sleep at all. I didn't need to look at the time, I knew it was four o'clock, and I just didn't want to get up. But I knew I had to, so I did.

I stood in the shower and let the water beat down on my back. Hot showers usually brought me to life–probably because I did my best thinking in the shower. But not this morning. This morning, all I could think about was getting back in the bed.

I heard the bathroom door open, and shortly there after, the shower door opened. "Mind if I join you?" she asked, and stepped in without waiting for my response. It wasn't like I was about to say no.

I moved a little to the side so she could get wet. "Not at all."

"I enjoyed you last night," Avonte said, and looked at me.

"What about this morning?"

"That was good, too. How are you feeling?"

"Just a little tired," I said.

"I know how to wake you up." Avonte dropped to her knees

and took my dick into her mouth like she was trying to swallow it all. It felt incredible, and I marveled at her skills. She was right, I was wide-awake now.

Avonte stood up and kissed me. Her tongue attacked mine, and I slid my hands from her breasts to her hips to her ass, and back up to her breasts again. I lowered my head and took her nipple into my mouth, and rolled it around with my tongue.

"Hmm," she said in a whisper. "I like it like that."

I nibbled on her neck and chin, and then I kissed her again. Then, I gently spread her legs and used my fingers to massage her clit and dip into her wetness. Avonte closed her eyes, and I felt her body tremble as I slid my fingers in and out of her. "You feel so good." Avonte told me and attacked my tongue. I lifted her off her feet and pulled myself into her.

As the hot water rained down on our skin, I bent my legs and pumped harder. Avonte rocked her hips, and I felt her juices flowing. "Yes, baby! Yes!"

After that, we took it back to the bed, and she finished me off. I got back in the shower, got dressed, and went home so I would be there when Taye woke up.

I met Avonte that evening at Belcourt on 4th Street. She sat quietly at the bar, sipping her drink and smiling. After dinner, we went back to Club Quarters. Once we were settled in our room, I turned to Avonte and took her in my arms.

"Devin, I left my purse in the car. Could you get it for me, please?"

"Whatever you want, baby."

"You called me baby," she beamed.

"Did I say something wrong?" I said sarcastically. I read her eyes and knew I hadn't.

"No," she replied firmly. "I like it."

"Maybe I should do it more often."

"Maybe you should just do that," she said with a bit of a bite.

Without any further hesitation, I left the room. Everything about her said, "Take me, Devin."

When I returned to the room with Avonte's purse, seeing the candles on both sides of the bed and hearing the music brought a smile to my face. Avonte emerged from the bathroom. I looked up. The sight of her, dressed in a black lace teddy, walking toward me, sent chills through me. "I like that."

"That's exactly what I had in mind," she replied, wrapping her arms around me.

I kissed her on the forehead.

"In fact, I think that you're overdressed."

"Really? What do you think I should be wearing?" I asked innocently, while Avonte unbuttoned my shirt and ran her hands across my chest.

"Nothing," she said, and kissed me.

I felt myself getting harder as I tasted her tongue. She undressed me slowly as we swayed to the music. She touched me in ways that I had only imagined she would. Avonte made slow circles around my nipples, and they began to harden. I removed the lace and revealed her breasts. I touched them, held them, squeezed them; teased them with my tongue. I glided my tongue around her beautiful dark circles, coming close, but never touching her nipples.

Avonte stroked my ever-hardening dick with long, even strokes from tip to shaft. My body shook. She squeezed my nipples, and her stroking became more intense, more focused.

Avonte spread her legs. I slid my hand along her thighs and gently fingered her clit. I felt it getting harder under my touch. Her head drifted back, and she moaned her approval. I felt her body quiver. I wanted to taste her, to drink from her fountain until I'd had my fill. I wanted to drown my face in an ocean of her come.

I watched her turn around and enjoyed the perfection that is her ass. Avonte lay down on her stomach. I sat beside her and ran my hands along her back, her perfect ass, and her firm thighs. I entered her from behind. Her pussy was so soft, so wet; I could barely control my passion. I felt her ass bucking, pounding against me. Avonte yelled, "FUCK ME HARDER!"

I did as she asked.

I felt the muscles inside her tighten.

I repositioned myself on the bed, and Avonte proceeded to lower her body onto my face. I ran my tongue along her lips, and then licked and sucked her clit. She moaned while continuing to slide her hand up and down my dick.

Once again, she lowered her head and took me into her mouth. My back arched. The movement of my tongue increased to a pace, which coincided with hers.

Her body shook.

"I don't want to come yet," she said, removing herself from my face and straddling my torso. She winked at me and lowered herself onto me. Taking my dick into the wetness between her thighs, we stared into each other's eyes and moved in unison—each movement agonizingly slow and deliberate to heighten our mutual pleasure.

After our first two nights together, I didn't see her for more than a week, but we talked every day. I felt guilty about cheating on Taye. I all but told her one night, but she was so deep into her depression that I don't really think she got what I was trying to say, or she just didn't care.

For the last five months that has been my life, I'd fuck Avonte all night, and then I'd go home. I'd wake up at seven o'clock in the morning in bed with Taye. Depending on how she was feeling that day, Taye would either start an argument with me, which happened a whole lot more than I'd like, or she'd ignore me totally, which was fine with me. I'd get dressed and then I'd go to work.

Over the past five months, I've grown less patient with Taye. I knew it was wrong, but that's the way I felt. It has gotten to the point where I can't stand to be around her, which led me to Avonte. She was like a drug. No matter how much I had her, I still wanted more. Avonte was always ready to give it to me, and it was always so fuckin' good. Avonte never let me leave her without coming first.

"I don't want you to have one drop left for her," she'd always say.

"You don't have to worry about that. She don't want none of this," I'd tell her.

"I know, but in case she comes to her senses one night, there won't be any left. This is my dick."

Each night we'd meet after work for dinner. One night, while we waited for our table, Avonte and I had drinks at the bar. We didn't even get seated at a table before we were out of there. Over drinks, we agreed that the only thing either of us was hungry for was each other. We went to the closest bed we could find, and fucked each other silly.

It was after 11 when I got home, and Taye was asleep, just as she was every night. I could set my clock by it. Every night at eight-thirty, Taye took her sleeping pills. By nine o'clock, she would be out like a light. That's how it began. Every night, I would come home and wait for Taye to pass out at nine. Then, I would leave the house and go be with Avonte, who'd be waiting at some motel near my house. We did our thing, and I'd be back in bed when Taye woke up.

As things between me and Taye got worse, I would come home less and less. Avonte and I would get together for dinner after I got off work. Someplace small and out of the way, where I was sure that I wouldn't be recognized. Some nights we'd hang out, take in a movie or a Broadway show, and other nights, it was straight to the hotel. It got to the point where I had spent so much on hotel rooms, that it was cheaper to rent a furnished studio apartment. I found a spot not too far from my job. When I got off work, Avonte would be there with dinner waiting. After dinner, we headed to the bedroom for the best sex I'd ever had. Then, about two or three in the morning, usually three, I'd leave Avonte and go home, so I could wake up next to Taye.

Avonte didn't like to talk about what was going on with her marriage, so I didn't ask. I didn't know how her husband let her be gone every night, all night, but I'm not complaining. Sometimes I wondered if Avonte was married at all, but here again, I ain't complaining.

It was Friday night, and I had gotten to the apartment a little earlier than I usually did. I found Avonte in the bed, curled up with her laptop, surfing the web. "Hi," she said when I came in the room.

"Hi, yourself," I said, and took off my jacket.

"I didn't feel like cooking tonight," Avonte said. "So, you're having me for dinner." She pulled back the covers. I loosened my tie and joined her in bed. You know what happened then. While we made love, I thought about what I was doing there. There I was, a married man, and I practically lived with Avonte. Avonte shook her hips and grabbed her breasts. "I can feel you getting harder inside me. Give me that juice, baby. I want it all."

My eyes and mouth opened wide, and my body became rigid. Avonte smiled then began pounding her body into mine, and rocking her hips furiously until she had taken it all from me. Avonte rolled off of me and lay flat on her back, out of breath, but smiling.

The two of us laid there for I don't know how long, in each other's arms, enjoying the quiet bliss after great sex. Avonte inched a little closer and kissed my chest. "You make me feel so good. Every time we do it, you take me to a new level."

"It is great. You make me feel good, too, Avonte."

"Let's do something tonight," Avonte said.

"Like what?"

"Since we got this place, we hardly do anything," she paused, while I gave her a funny look, and then she continued, "other than fuck, I mean."

"What did you have in mind?"

"I don't know. What do you wanna do?"

I've always hated that. Why do women do that? They wanna go out, but when you ask them where, they never have a clue. I decided to turn the tables on her. I sat up in bed and looked at Avonte. "I don't know. What do *you* wanna do?"

Avonte laughed. "I tell you what."

"What?" I said, and kissed her. I couldn't get enough of her.

"Why don't we take a shower and get dressed. We'll figure it out from there."

"I'm hungry, are you?"

"Of course," Avonte said, and rolled out of bed.

"So, we know eating is involved in this plan. Maybe if you put on something real sexy, I might take you dancing."

"Really? We haven't been dancing since San Juan. Sounds like a plan is coming together."

Once we were dressed, we had dinner at Bocca's on East 19th Street. It's a Roman restaurant that we'd been promising to try. And I have to say that in a city like New York where you can find Italian food on just about every corner, the Roman cuisine was outstanding.

Since Avonte wore something sexy as I requested, after dinner, we went dancing. We had been on the dance floor from the time we hit the door. Both of us loved dancing, and we had so much fun dirty dancing the night away. When Avonte said that she was tired, we left the floor. "I'm gonna get a drink."

"I'm going to the men's room. Why don't you order me a drink, and I'll meet you at the bar."

While I was in there, I took out my cell phone, and just as I did every night, I blocked my number and called my house to see if Taye would answer. She never did. Sometimes I wished she would answer when I called. That would mean she didn't take her sleeping pills, which could've been an indication she was getting better.

I really did want her to get better. There was still some part of me that remembered the beautiful life we were building together. There was that part of me that still loved her, and hated to see her so depressed. But lately, that voice had been silenced by parts of me that couldn't stand to be around her. I began to enjoy my newfound freedom, and was in no real hurry to give it up.

I washed my hands and came out of the men's room, and had begun making my way to the bar to join Avonte, when I saw a woman. The way her jet-black hair kept dropping over her pretty face made her look kind of innocent, yet very sexy at the same time. She was a tall woman, slender, but not skinny. She had nice-sized tits, and a bubble butt that made me want to follow her, so I did. She walked around the club for a while, obviously looking for somebody who she couldn't find. When she stopped and looked around again, I stepped to her.

"Hello," I said over the music.

"Hi," she said, and continued to look around.

"You're very pretty."

"Thank you," she said, and looked at me for the first time. A smile crept across her lips.

I leaned forward and asked, "What's your name?"

"Angel," she answered in a voice that sounded like it belonged to an angel.

"My name is Devin."

Angel held out her hand. "Nice to meet you, Devin."

"Believe me, Angel, the pleasure is all mine," I said and took her in with my eyes. "I couldn't help but notice that you seem to be looking for somebody."

"Yeah," Angel said, and looked around the club again. "I was supposed to be meeting a friend here, but I guess she's not gonna show."

"Did you try calling her to see if she was coming?"

"No, she doesn't have a cell phone," Angel said, and sighed deeply.

"You mean that there are still people in New York who don't have cells?"

"I don't know about all that, but she sure doesn't." Angel took another deep breath. "I think I've waited long enough for her."

"I don't think anybody who looks like you should be kept waiting."

"I can't argue with your logic, so I'm going home," Angel said, and started for the door.

I walked along side her. "Listen, I would like to see you again. Maybe we could get together some time and have a drink."

Angel stopped walking and faced me. She looked me up and down then tilted her head. "I'd like that," she said, and dug around in her purse for a pen, and something to write her number on.

We exchanged numbers and said goodbye, with a promise that we would be in touch with each other soon.

Once I saw Angel leave the club, I went to the bar to join Avonte. It was getting late, and I wanted to fuck her one more time before I went home. As I got closer to the bar, I saw Avonte standing there. And standing right next to her was another cutie dressed in dark purple leather. She was about the same height and build as Avonte. But where Avonte's hair is short, this woman had long, black hair that was parted in the middle, and hung down the middle of her back. Her dark completion and dark eyes made her very sexy. Even though I was happy with the sex I was having with Avonte, I wanted her, too.

Chapter Fourteen

Avonte

I waited by the bar for what seemed like a long time, waiting for Devin to come back from the bathroom. I looked around the club, but I didn't see him anywhere. I took sip of my drink and moved to the beat of the music, thinking about how I was enjoying my new life. I was finally living life on my own terms, and I wanted to experience it all. I wanted to experience everything that life had to offer. Devin was a big part of that. I especially liked the way he treated me, and the way he made me feel. Devin treated me like I was a queen, and when we made love, it was like nothing I've ever experienced.

I enjoyed my life with Devin. We saw each other practically every day. After spending so much money on hotels, Devin decided to rent a small apartment close to his job. We'd spend the rest of the night together until I drained Devin, and send him home to sleep with his wife. Most days, I'd leave when he left and go back to my apartment

I still hadn't told him very much about myself. At times, I felt bad about that, but I liked the way things were with Devin. I didn't want to spoil things by dragging all that money into it. I knew from experience that money had a way of changing people. Making them do things that under normal circumstances, they wouldn't even consider.

I took another sip of my drink and wondered what was taking Devin so long. "Hello," a female voice said to me.

I turned to see a woman standing next to me, wearing a dark purple leather jumpsuit that zipped in the front, which she used to display a healthy cleavage. "Hi."

"That's a real nice dress you're wearin'. Where'd you get it?" the woman asked.

"Saks."

I have to say, she was wearin' the hell out of that leather, but I wasn't about to tell her that. I turned away and took another sip of my drink. "Saks, huh?" the woman asked. "You gotta have wild dough to shop there."

"Actually, it was a gift."

"Yeah, you got it like that," she said, and looked me over. "What you think?" she said, and held out her arms. "You think I could get some nigga to drop nice shit like that on me?"

I finished my drink and signaled for the bartender, before I gave her an answer. "Honey, the way you're wearing that leather, I'm sure getting men to do what you want is not your problem in life."

She put her hands on her breasts. "You think?" she asked.

We both laughed, and I knew she was trying to hit on me. I looked at her again. I could tell that she was a little on the ghetto side, but she was a beautiful woman, and sexy as hell. I've never told anybody this, not even Tyrone, but I'd been with a woman before. I never told anybody about my lesbian freshmen year.

Her name was Amy Cranston. She was my roommate. She was a gorgeous blonde from California. They used to call her Everybody Wants Amy, because every boy on campus wanted her. One weekend during first quarter, we had both just gotten back to the room from different parties. We were both a little drunk, and were talking and giggling about the night we'd had.

After a while, I got up and started getting undressed to get ready for bed. Those days, I slept in a big T-shirt and panties. I didn't really think anything of it when Amy stopped talking as I took off my bra. Once I was in the bed, she stood up. "Avonte."

"Yes, Amy."

"There's something I just gotta tell you. Something I've wanted to tell you since I got here."

"What now, Amy?"

When she started taking off her clothes, once again, I didn't think anything of it, until she came and sat down on the bed next to me. "Avonte, I'm a lesbian," Amy said, giggling. She slid her hand under the cover and began rubbing my thigh. "And I've wanted you since I walked in this room."

I lay there paralyzed and in shook. My roommate, Everybody Wants Amy, was easing my panties to one side, and I felt her finger on my clit.

"I've never done anything like this before," I mumbled. "I mean with a girl."

Amy eased the covers off of my body, and began lowering her head. "Just relax, Avonte. You don't have to do anything."

My secret relationship with Amy lasted for the rest of the school year. During the summer, she transferred to UCLA, and we never communicated after that. Since then, I hadn't been approached by any other woman. That is, until now.

"So, what's you're name?" she asked.

"Avonte," I said, thinking that there was no harm in talking to her.

"Qianna Patterson," she said, and held out her hand.

"Good to meet you?"

"So, uh, let me ask you a question; you here by yourself?"

"No, I came here with somebody. He's gone to the men's room."

"That's too bad." Qianna took a step closer to me.

"Why's that?" I asked, knowing what she'd say.

"'Cause you and me coulda had some fun together," Qianna said, as Devin finally came to the bar.

"Hey," Devin said, and kissed me on the cheek. "Did you miss me?"

"Yes, baby. I was starting to get a little worried."

"I ran into an old friend from college."

"Where is he? I'd like to meet him."

"He left," Devin said quickly, and pointed at his drink. "This me?"

"Yes. That should tell you how long you've been gone. Your ice has started to melt."

"I'm sorry, Avonte. I promise to make it up to you later."

"Is that your man?"

"Yes." I turned to Devin. "Baby, I want you to meet somebody. This is Qianna. Qianna, this is Devin."

Devin smiled. "Nice to meet you."

"Good to meet you, too, Devin," Qianna said, shaking his hand.

"I'd buy you ladies a drink, if I could ever get this guy's attention," Devin said, and tried in vain to get the bartender's attention.

When Devin turned away, Qianna leaned to me and whispered. "He's kinda cute. You should see if he wanna play with us."

"I don't remember saying that I wanted to play."

"Oh, you wanna play with me, brown sugar," Qianna said, and eased her hand between my thighs. I felt like I was back in college that first time with Amy. It felt like a current of electricity had shot through my body. I thought about the promise I made to start experiencing everything that life had to offer. "Go ahead. Ask him. I bet he'll be down for it."

She was right about both of us. I wanted to play with her, and Devin was definitely down for it. It just took me a while to get up the courage to ask him.

When we got to the apartment, as soon as we walked through the door, Qianna ran her hand across Devin's leg. She grabbed Devin's face and kissed him. Devin stroked my thighs, and I unzipped his pants. Devin stepped out of his pants and immediately went right back at Qianna. I was beginning to get a little jealous that he was showing her so much attention, but I had to remind myself that it was my idea to do this.

As quickly as I could, I took off my dress. "Damn, you fine as hell," Qianna said, and began sucking my nipple.

"Ain't she," Devin said, and attacked the other nipple.

Soon, we all were naked and had eased our way onto the couch. I took one of Qianna's nipples into my mouth, and Devin quickly went for the other. Qianna leaned back and held Devin's head in place with one hand, and squeezed her breast, while I licked and sucked the other.

Qianna looked down at me while I gently sucked her nipple. "Come here. I wanna taste you."

I stood up on the couch and lowered myself to her face. Qianna spread my lips while she made circles around my clit. She slid her tongue inside me and sucked my lips. She was rough, but it was turning me the fuck on. It wasn't easy, but I steadied myself against the wall. I felt my body begin to tremble as she sucked my clit, and licked it with the tip of her tongue. I looked back at Devin. He had crawled between her legs and was making Qianna quiver in ecstasy with his finger, and his tongue.

Qianna sucked my clit and it grew harder. I began to feel my body convulse, so I got down from there. "Where you think you goin with that sweet pussy?"

"To the bed."

Qianna pushed Devin's head out of the way and followed behind me. Devin wasn't far behind. I laid across the bed and spread my legs. Qianna literally dove in between them. Devin quickly got in behind her, pulled her hips up and thrust himself inside her. "Oh! You got a big dick. Let's see if you know how to use it."

I lay there in complete ecstasy, while Qianna worked magic with her tongue. I got so turned on watching Devin slam his body into Qianna, squeezing my nipples, while she feasted on me. Devin pulled completely out of her, and then slammed himself into her again. When he was inside her, Devin smacked her ass as hard as he could. Qianna lifted her head from between my thighs long enough to say, "That's right, nigga. Get that pussy."

Qianna took two fingers to her lips and moistened them. Then, she slid them inside me and zoned in on my G-spot.

"You like that?" she asked.

I closed my eyes and started thrusting myself onto her hand. Qianna had me dripping wet—wetter than I've ever been—man or woman.

I looked at Devin, his eyes were closed, and he was pumping away. I could tell by the way he was breathing that he was about to come. I guess Qianna could tell it, too. "Don't you bust that nut inside me. Come on my ass."

After a few more hard stokes, Devin pulled out of her and sprayed her cheeks. When he was done, Qianna spun around and took Devin into her mouth. I gently massaged my swollen lips, while I watched Qianna sucking and stroking him. Once his dick was firm again, Qianna turned around, put his dick back inside her, and then dropped her head between my thighs.

Qianna licked me with the tip of her tongue. When she slid her tongue inside me, she sucked my clit until it grew harder, and my body began to quiver. "Oooh shit!"

Chapter Fifteen

Qianna

Jackpot!

That's all I can fuckin' say. All that good-ass pussy Avonte carryin' around between them thighs, and that horse dick Devin got, shit. And judging from that big-ass rock on Avonte's finger, they got money, too. I hit the fuckin' jackpot.

Yeah, I could tell by the way Avonte looked at me when I grabbed these titties, that she was wit' it. And you show me a man that ain't down for sex wit' two women, and I'll show you a faggot.

I knew that he would, but I guess Avonte didn't 'cause that bitch assed around for over an hour before she even got around to askin'. But it was cool. The three of us hung out, drank, danced, and had a good time. My boy Devin was steady buyin' drinks like they was water.

It was like the nigga was tryin' to get us drunk so he could fuck both of us. I had to laugh 'cause the shit was on, and he didn't even know it. He coulda saved that money, or better yet, he coulda handed that shit to me. Shit, I was 'bout to tell him the deal myself, when Avonte finally told him.

We were all on the floor dancin' together, and me and Avonte had that nigga sandwiched in like a burger. I was in front of him and Avonte was behind. I can still see the way his facial expression changed when she whispered that shit in his ear. "What?" he asked. Then she told him again, and his eyes opened wide.

That nigga's neck snapped 'round and he looked at Avonte, then that neck snapped again, and he looked at me. I smiled and stuck out my tongue.

"Hell yeah! Let's get the fuck outta here," Devin said, and dragged us off the floor.

I had hit the fuckin' jackpot! Not bad for a bitch four weeks out of Bedford Hills Correctional Facility for Women. To be honest, this was exactly what I'd been visualizing ever since I saw them talkin' 'bout *The Secret* on Oprah.

Every night after lights out, I'd lie in bed and visualize; I would visualize myself havin' good sex and plenty of money. I'd see myself at the mall tryin' shit on, then goin' to the register and payin' for it. I'd see myself walkin' through the mall with my arms fulla bags of shit I bought. I'd see myself at the clubs, dressed in my new shit, turnin' every head, man and woman, in the club. I would see myself on airplanes, flyin' to the islands and shit for the weekend. I was feelin' so fuckin' good after visualizing all that shit, that I'd start playin' wit' myself. Then, I would visualize me havin' good sex.

Avonte pushed my head away from her, and I rolled over on my back, and she quickly crawled between my legs. Avonte reached between my thighs and fingered my clit with one hand, while she squeezed her breast with the other.

Devin stood over me and I stroked himself, and I took him

into my mouth again. I liked suckin' his dick. Avonte very deliberately spread my lips and sucked my clit, but the whole time, she was staring at Devin. Avonte slid her tongue inside me, and sucked my moist lips gently. I felt her body quiver as Avonte licked my clit with the tip of her tongue. Avonte sucked my clit and it grew harder. My thighs pressed together and my body convulsed.

Devin looked down at Avonte's ass up in the air, and stepped away from me. He fell in behind her, held onto her hips, and entered her slowly. He got into a long, rhythmic stroke, while he watched me squeeze my nipples. Devin pulled almost completely out of Avonte, and then slowly entered her again.

As Devin lay down, Avonte lay next to him, gliding her hand up and down his erection. I got up on the bed and lowered myself onto Devin's face. He reached up with his hands, and ran them across my titties. He ran his tongue along my lips and started to lick my clit.

I watched Avonte gliding her hands across his skin to his now throbbing hardness, and slowly begin to massage it. She straddled his torso and eased herself down on it. She moaned her pleasure while continuing to slide up and down his dick. I rested my titties gently on Avonte's back, cupped my hands under her titties, and squeezed her nipples, while I nibbled and sucked on her neck and shoulder.

Avonte repositioned herself on his dick, so she would be facing me. We kissed and explored each other's bodies with our hands. As Devin licked and sucked my dripping wet pussy, he pushed himself as deep as he could inside Avonte.

Devin made me come, and Avonte came right behind me. We both lay down on either side of Devin. He was still rock hard. Devin began kissing Avonte, and I started strokin' his dick and squeezing his balls. Then I took Devin into my mouth. Avonte got up on her knees and ran her hands over my body. She started from my ankle then rubbed along my leg. Then she joined me between Devin's legs. "Let me have some of that," Avonte said.

"It's big enough to share," I mumbled. We made him come hard. Avonte took Devin's face into her hands and kissed him. I watched them kissing and ran my hands over my body. Devin was watchin' me squeezin' my nipples and fingerin' myself. He eased away from Avonte's lips, crawled over her, and took one of my nipples into his mouth. I leaned back and held his head in place with one hand, and squeezed my nipple with the other. Avonte moved my hand out of the way and began suckin' my nipple. Yeah, this is the shit.

With my newfound friends, Avonte on my right nipple, and my boy Devin suckin' like a greedy crack fiend on the other nipple, that old temper of mine was a thing of the past. From now on, it would be nothin' but good sex for me.

Chapter Sixteen

Devin

In-fuckin'-credible. I can't think of any other words that could describe it. Fuckin' Avonte and Qianna Patterson was in-fuckin'-credible. I had been with two women once before, but it wasn't like this. That time I was so excited, I came before it really got wild.

This shit was off the chain. And Avonte, there is more to her than she's been saying, that was for sure. You can't tell me that it was her first time eating pussy. I couldn't wait to get back to them later that night. Both of them called me during the day wanting to get together again, but I couldn't get away.

I had too much work to do at the office. And on top of that, Sandra hadn't been to work in over a week, and she hadn't called either. I kind of expected something like that would happen after what happened between us. Sandra and I had had sex again while we were working late one night last week, after everybody was gone. Or at least we thought everybody was gone. I was sitting in my chair behind the desk. Sandra was standing up with her hands on the desk, and I was pumping away, when we heard a key hit the lock. She got off of me and had just pulled up her pants, when the cleaning lady walked in on us. We could tell by the look on her face that she knew what we were doing.

Sandra left that night embarrassed as hell, but I just never expected it to last all week. I figured a day or two to get over it, and she'd be all right and ready to work. But that wasn't the case. It was Friday, and I hadn't heard from her, nor had she returned any of my calls. I'd covered for her to this point. The only one who really made an issue about it was Winston. He was making a pest of himself. I knew that soon, and very soon, I'd be forced to make a decision. I would have to fire her for abandonment of her position.

I rolled into the driveway expecting to see Taye's car, but she wasn't home yet. I went in the house and grabbed a brew from the fridge. The phone rang. I started not to answer it, but I did.

"Hello."

"Devin."

"Sandra?"

"It's me. I know you're mad at me, and you probably fired me by now, but–"

I cut her off. "No, I didn't fire you, and no, I'm not mad at you. I really just wanted to know if you were all right."

"I'm fine."

"You sure?"

"Really, Devin, I'm fine. I just had some things that I had to workout for myself."

"And?"

"And I faxed you my resignation. It should be there when you get there Monday morning. But I thought that you deserved better than that."

"Wait a minute, Sandra; you're resigning because of what happened between us?"

"Not just that, Devin, it's a lot of things, but yeah, that's a major part of it. I can't come to work and see you everyday, knowing what a fool I've been making of myself."

"You haven't been making a fool of yourself, Sandra. It was just something that happened, we didn't intend for it to happen, it just did. But it's not worth giving up your job for. Please, Sandra, take a few more days and think about it."

"I have thought about it, and I know this is what I have to do. Me and Ike talked about it, and we're going to move back to Texas, so if nothing else, he's happy about that."

"How do you feel about it?"

"It's the only way it could happen. To be honest with you, Devin, it didn't just happen. I came in your office that first night with a plan. You just played right into it."

"What?"

"I've always wanted you, Devin. I just never gave into my feelings or acted on them, until that first night. Since that night, I've tried my best to act like it didn't happen; like I didn't want to feel you inside me every time we were alone. But I had to stop lying to myself. I know that I can't face you, not any more."

I sat there in shock holding the phone. I never knew she felt that way; never had any idea that I was being seduced that night. But it's like Taye told me once, "Y'all just stupid that way."

While we're down here scheming on level one, a woman is on level five, running a program that our dumb asses could never even imagine.

I thought I heard a noise.

I looked around for Taye.

"Devin, you still there?"

"Yeah, Sandra, I'm still here. Look, it shouldn't have happened. It will never happen again. I like you, Sandra, but it's not like that for me." I thought for a minute about what I was doing with Avonte and Qianna. Compared to that, what I had done with Sandra didn't even rate.

"That's why I gotta go. You can see that, can't you?"

"Yeah, I understand. I hate to lose you. But I understand you feeling like its the best thing for everybody."

Now I was glad she was leaving. That would be the last thing I needed. I didn't want, nor need, that type of pressure on my job. I had more than enough going on already. "Well, give me a call before you go."

This time I was sure I heard something.

"I can't promise you that I will, but I'll be thinking about you, Devin. Good-bye." Without another word, Sandra hung up the phone. I hated to lose Sandra. It would be like cutting off my right hand, but I would gladly sacrifice it. Sandra could be replaced.

I went to see if Taye was home and to get another brew, maybe something a little stronger to go with it. I definitely could use it. I went into the kitchen and got a bottle of beer, and headed for the bar in the living room to get a drink. I poured a drink.

"You wanna tell me about it?" Taye said, sitting quietly on the couch. The tears rolling down her cheeks let me know that she had heard the incriminating parts of my conversation. I shot my drink and poured another one, before I turned to face her again. She looked at me. The pain she must have been feeling shot through me faster than the drink.

"I know it sounds bad," I said, and thought that I should have ended that call when I first thought I'd heard something. *Y'all just stupid that way.* "But it's not what you think."

I sat down on the couch next to her and reached for her hand. Taye jerked it back quickly. "Don't touch me, Devin!" she yelled. "You're messin' around on me!" She started to cry. "How could you?"

"Don't cry, Taye, please. I didn't do anything," I lied quickly and reached out for her. I wanted to wipe away her tears, hold her, and tell that I loved her. But she turned away.

She wiped away her own tears. "How can you sit there and tell me you didn't do anything? I heard you." Taye looked into my eyes. "I heard you say, 'It shouldn't have happened'." Her expression and tone had changed from hurt to anger.

"I know what I said, but just let me explain."

"What's there to explain, Devin? Huh? Tell me, what you got to explain. What could you possibly say? I heard you!"

Taye got up and so did I. "Let me tell you what happened."

She looked at me and rolled her eyes.

"Let me tell you what happened, and you'll see that I didn't do anything," I said, working on the lie I was about to tell her.

"Okay, Devin, I'm listening."

Taye sat down, folded her arms, and gave me a look that let me know that no matter what I said, she wouldn't believe me.

But I went for it anyway.

As calmly as I could, I told her the story of me and Sandra. How I gave her a massage that went too far, but I swore that was all that happened. I knew I should have come up with something better than the near truth, but it was all I could think of.

"Bullshit!" was Taye's response.

"Believe me, baby, that's exactly how it happened."

"I should have known something was going on!" Taye yelled. "All those late nights you've been having lately."

"I've been at work," I got up and walked over to the bar. I definitely needed another drink.

"Stop lying to me!" Taye yelled, and the tears began again. "I called your office–more than once; and never got an answer. Then you come home at ridiculous hours of the morning, do what you want to me, and then run to the shower."

"What are you talkin' about?"

"You forced yourself on me!"

"What are you talking about?" I never forced myself on her. Taye was really losing her mind.

"I know you thought that I was sleeping, but I know when you come in! You dirty fucking bastard! How could you?"

She was right about that. I thought that with the amount of sleeping pills she was taking, she couldn't have been awake to catch me. And if she was awake, why didn't she say anything? "Taye, please, calm down. Nothing happened."

"Stop lying to me!" Taye screamed, and threw a lamp at me. I ducked before it hit me.

"You know you're fucking that woman. The least you could do is to be man enough to admit it."

I've always wondered why at times like this, women always wanna question your manhood?

"There's nothing to admit. Nothing happened for me to admit to. I did not have sex with Sandra."

Taye didn't say anything for a second. Then her eyes narrowed.

"Ain't Sandra that country-ass bony woman you work with?"

"Think about what you just said. You know I don't like skinny women." I fired back quickly. It was the first bit of truth that I could fit in. Taye knew how my taste in women ran, and Sandra didn't fit the build.

Avonte and Qianna were another story. Both of them were just the right size. In so many ways, they were both built like Taye. The truth was, if she hadn't shut off that part of our life, none of this would be happening.

"Taye, I don't want Sandra." And I really didn't. "I don't want anybody but you. Taye, please let's both just calm down so we can talk about this. Don't do this to me." Just short of getting down on my knees. "I love you."

"I know you didn't want her bony ass!" Taye screamed and grabbed the candy dish from the coffee table, and hurled it in my direction.

Taye got up and started walking toward the kitchen, and I was right in trail. Once she got in the kitchen, she started taking things out to cook for dinner. Then without any warning, Taye began breaking dishes, and throwing pots and pans around the kitchen. She wasn't throwing them in my direction, but she kept screaming that I was a lying bastard, and how she knew I had fucked Sandra.

Then as quickly as her rage began, it ended. I looked at Taye as she stood there like she was in a trance. Then she said, "I have no one to blame but myself," she said softly.

Then she looked around the kitchen and began quietly cleaning up the mess she'd made. While Taye picked up the pots and pans, I grabbed the bloom and swept up the broken dishes.

Once the kitchen was in some semblance of order, Taye began cooking. I stood there watching her, confused, but not surprised. She likes to cook. Maybe it was therapy. Maybe it was escapism. I had no way of knowing, because she wasn't talking. I don't know how many times or how many variations of '*Say something*' ran through my mind, but I wasn't giving up.

I had to get her to talk to me. I had to know where she was. What she was thinking. After she finished cooking, she said, "I left the food out, you can fix yourself something if you want to," without looking at me. The tone of her voice made me desperate to know what was going on in her mind.

So I talked.

I talked about anything I could think of that she might comment on. The weather, politics, I even tried my hand at religion. Taye sat at the table quietly eating. She did get up and say, "Excuse me." But that was only because I was standing in front of the refrigerator, and she wanted a glass of water with dinner. She sat back down at the table and continued eating, and I continued talking. When she got finished eating, Taye started to walk out of the kitchen, but she stopped. "I hate you. I don't ever want to hear your voice again."

Chapter Seventeen

Avonte

When I felt her lips touch mine, the indescribable feeling of our lips intertwining felt so good. Qianna was a little rough at first, and then she began to nibble softly on them. I thought I would lose my mind the way she tugged on my bottom lip, and held it between hers. It got my river flowing, and I hoped that she would slide her body between my legs and suck me dry.

She grabbed my breasts and squeezed them hard, slapped them, and then eased it up with soft, tender stokes. Qianna was driving me crazy.

She used her tongue to make circles around my nipples. As Qianna bit at my nipples, she used her fingers and slid them in and out of the wetness between my thighs. She alternated back and forth between squeezing my nipples and fingering my clit, while she continued to penetrate me with her fingers. I spread my legs a bit wider, and Qianna parted my lips. She began using her wet tongue to flicker back and forth across my clit.

I laid there watching Qianna, this beautiful woman, with her face buried between my thighs. I was overwhelmed by the way she held my clit between her lips, and all but attacked it in ways that no man ever had or could.

I held her head in place, and tried in vain to control the pleasure Qianna was giving me. I didn't want her to go too fast or too slow, because I never wanted the feeling to end.

I laid spread eagle on the bed, and grabbed the bedposts tightly as Qianna moaned, sending a tickling sensation through my swollen clit. I held my nipples and closed my eyes as the river flowed again. "Oh shit," I screamed.

Qianna lifted her head and smiled at me, before attacking my drenched pussy again. Spitting and holding my clit between her fingers. "That's it bitch. Come all over me!"

"Yes, yes!" I cried, and quickly guided her head back toward my clit. "I'm gonna come!" I yelled and screamed my pleasure, as Qianna moaned and plunged her fingers deeper inside me.

At that point, I couldn't take anymore and rolled away from her, or at least I tried. Qianna grabbed me back, and once again, buried her head between my come-drenched thighs. Then she flipped me over and I literally mounted her face.

"You are so fuckin' hot, Avonte," Qianna said, and pulled me down on her.

I tried to speak as her tongue slid in and out of me, and her finger massaged my clit, but no words came out. Her touch was suddenly soft and gentle, but firm at the same time. I felt waves of current emanating from my clit that spread throughout my body. I reached for the wall to steady myself, and my body shuddered from the inside out.

Qianna smiled and lightly spanked my ass. As my hands dropped to her breasts, she spread my cheeks and slowly slid two fingers in, inching deeper and deeper inside me. The deeper she got, the wetter I got. I held on to the headboard, mumbling my pleasure and caressing my breasts, and I came again.

Hard.

I forced myself to pull away from her. I rolled off of her and she rolled on top of me. Qianna kissed my lips and then slid her body along mine, and allowed our lips to slide up and down on each other.

All I could do was moan at the site of Qianna sliding her body against mine. The feeling of her breasts against mine made my nipples swell. And when she slid her nipples over mine, I nearly lost my mind. Once again, her fingers found their mark between my legs; they slid effortlessly across my lips, occasionally finding their way to my clit.

I massaged her breasts, gently squeezing her nipples, and started kissing and licking her neck, sucking and gently biting at her earlobes. When my index finger found her clit, Qianna's eyes and mouth both opened wide. "About fuckin' time."

She laid spread eagle across the bed, and I crawled across the bed to her. Qianna didn't move at first, she seemed very content watching me finger her, and sucking her clit. My pace was slow and steady, it was almost musical.

"Bring that wet pussy here. Let a bitch suck it," Qianna demanded.

I maneuvered around as quickly as I could, and lowered myself to her waiting tongue. I closed my eyes, enjoying the feeling of her fingers inside me, and the pleasure we were giving each other. The feeling of her two fingers excited me. My hips shook, and I began to quiver from the inside. I stopped moving to try and keep from coming again, but I couldn't.

My entire body was quivering uncontrollably. I got off of her, but Qianna grabbed my head, pushed it between her legs, and held it tight. I fingered myself furiously, and my excitement only proved to intensify the motion of my tongue against her clit. She began to move with me. When I felt her clit throb, I knew she was no longer able to control herself.

"Yes, shit yes!" she screamed. Her face twisted and contoured. Her body became ridged. I sucked her clit and pumped my fingers harder. Qianna's mouth was open; her eyes were locked in mine now. I knew I had Qianna just like she had me.

I rolled away from Qianna and rolled into the fetal position at the bottom bed. I lay there with my eyes closed tight, holding myself. I opened my eyes when I felt the bed move. Qianna got up and began picking up her clothes, and I prayed she wasn't leaving.

"You mind if I smoke?" she asked, and held up a pack of cigarettes.

"I'd rather you didn't, but go ahead," I said, feeling too good to be worried about anything so trivial.

"This a nice place," Qianna said, and sat down on the bed near me. "This you?"

I nodded my head. "Yes." It was all I could manage after the way she'd drained me.

"So whose place was we at last night?"

"That's Devin's little a hideaway."

"We shoulda came here." Qianna spread out across the bed and took a drag of her cigarette. "Bigger bed."

"Devin doesn't know about this place."

"He doesn't? Now I'm confused."

"Devin doesn't know about this place because he thinks I'm

still living with my husband."

"I thought y'all was married."

"No. At least not to each other."

"That's why he rolled out of there so quick last night; had to get home to his wife." Qianna took my hand. "That why you ain't wearin' that rock you had on last night?"

"Yes," I said quietly, and gently pulled my hand back. "The only time I wear it is when I'm with him. I take it off as soon as I get here."

"What's up with that?"

"I came home one day and found my husband with another woman, so I left him."

"What that got to do wit' you not tellin' Devin?"

"When I met him I wasn't feeling too good about myself. Like I said, I had just caught my husband with a younger woman, and I was feeling old and unattractive," I admitted to her, and wondered why I was being so honest with a woman I had just met the night before. "Tyrone, that's my husband, he had me thinking that all I ever had going for me was his money."

"Oooh, so, y'all rich, huh?"

"Not rich, but we were all right."

"Your bitch-ass is rich," Qianna said, and pushed my legs open. "I can tell by the way you carry it."

"Anyway, when I met Devin, and he wanted me for me, just me, I didn't want it to change because of money," I explained while she fingered my clit. "I thought about telling him, but every time I think of it, it never seems like the right time to say, 'Hey, I been lying to you all these months'."

For the next couple of months, I saw Qianna just about every day. I simply couldn't get enough of her. As for Devin, I've been avoiding him. I've only seen him maybe five times since that first night with Qianna, and three of those times, she was with me. I don't really think that it bothered him. I think he likes fuckin' Qianna more than he likes fuckin' me. I can't honestly say that I blame him. After making love to Qianna, I had basically lost all interest in having sex with a man.

Chapter Eighteen

Qianna

Let me tell you something. Things couldn't be any better for me if this was a movie, and I was writtin' the shit myself. I got Devin and Avonte both so sprung on this pussy, it ain't even funny no more. I got them both spendin' crazy money on me'; buyin' me anything I even think I want. Clothes, shoes, jewelry, digital camera, iPod; all that shit. And Devin makes sure I always got plenty of weed. Both of 'em hittin' me off with cash. Plus, I got a couple of other little slim cuties, one that does things to me with a strap that makes me shake.

It was wonderful.

But if it was a competition and I had to pick a winner, it would be Avonte. For one, her pockets are deeper than Devin's, and two, her self-esteem issues make her easy for me to control. Avonte needs the approval of the people she feels close to, so she will do anything to please me. Probably some childhood shit about her daddy.

See, I knew payin' attention in group while I was at Bedford, listenin' to them dumb bitches talk about their problems would pay off.

Avonte has problems with men. She never really trusted Devin. That's why she didn't tell him she got money. Fuck all that bullshit she tried to run on me about her wantin' him to want her for her.

Bullshit!

It was all about the money. And now that she caught hubby cheatin', in her eyes, men are fucked.

So she's been avoiding Devin for weeks. The three of us hooked up a few of times. But other than that, Avonte don't want to be bothered with him. After a while, he took the hint and stopped calling her.

Now, there wasn't any point in letting all that fat, juicy dick go to waste, so when he calls me, I come. He always makes it worth my time, and I make it worth his. Devin called me and said he wanted us to get together that evening before he went home.

I feel sorry for Devin sometimes. I know that he was really into Avonte, and her avoidin' him hurts his ass. He told me about his wife's issues, and that she was gettin' worse. He was trying to be home with her more often. But he just had to have some of this wet shit I got here, so I met him at his apartment and we fucked.

I felt my nipples stiffen as they bounced into the bed. When Devin spanked my thigh, the sensation turned me on. The sound of him slidin' in and out of me made me wetter.

Devin grabbed me by the shoulders, and pulled my body into his. I started twistin' my hips, and he started rubbing my thighs and my ass at the same time. Then he stopped and took a few steps back. "What the hell are you doin'?"

I turned around and watched Devin stroking his length, still wonderin' why he had stopped. I rubbed my hands over my tits. I ran my hands up to my neck and back down to my stiff and very sensitive nipples. Then I squeezed them between my fingers, and watched Devin stoke himself. Without a word, I fell to my knees and took Devin into my mouth.

"Damn," Devin hollered, and stumbled back onto a nearby chair. I laughed at his ass and stepped to him, spread my legs wide, and pushed my fuckin' titties in his face.

He sucked my nipples. He had his eyes open, watching me watching him. I watched as his tongue moved around these chocolate covered raisins. I began playing with the other one. Devin pulled back, and started watching me.

"You like what you see, nigga?" I asked, moving my hand between my thighs.

Devin didn't answer; he just palmed my titties and squeezed them. I put my hand on his shoulder to steady myself, and swung one leg over and mounted him.

I started shaking my hips and rubbing my titties again. Taking a finger into my mouth, tracing from my lips to my chin, then down to my neck, and then to my belly button.

As I bounced up and down on him, I twisted my hips, rocking them from left to right. Then I spread my legs even farther apart, and bent my knees slightly so I could shake my ass up and down on his dick.

Devin held me close, and moved his hips in sync with my rhythm. I could tell by the look in his eyes that he could feel my walls tightening and loosening around him.

"You love this pussy, don't you?" I said, as I rotated between a bounce and grind move that was drivin' him crazy. "Yeah, that's it, come for me," I instructed, since he was wearin' a condom. "I want to feel you explode inside me."

Devin moved his hips and tried to pump himself into me as hard as he could. I matched his every move, stroke for stroke. I felt him begin to expand inside me, and I fucked him harder, movin' my hips even faster and harder.

Devin grabbed my waist and tried to slow my roll, but that wasn't happenin'. We both collapsed in each other's arms.

That shit was so fuckin' good. But this particular night, Devin wasn't quite himself. I could tell that wife shit was wearin' on him.

When he was done, instead of getting out of bed and runnin' for the shower like he always did, Devin just laid there starin' at the ceiling.

"What's wrong with you?"

"I don't wanna go home."

"Wifey trippin' again?"

"I never know what to expect when I get there. Either she'll be practically catatonic, or she'll be mad enough to kill me about some shit I know nothing about."

"That's fucked up."

"Tell me about it. I don't know how much more I can take."

"Why don't you kill her and be done wit' that shit."

"That's a good idea. Yeah, that's it, just kill her, then I'll be in jail. No thanks."

"Okay, but if she was fuckin' wit' me like she fuckin' wit' you—shit—I'd have to kill her ass. Life is too fuckin' short to be goin' through no fuckin' changes."

"You're right about that."

"Of course I'm right. You kill her ass and then you'll have some peace."

"Just like that?"

"Just like that."

"If it's so easy, then why don't you kill her for me?"

"How much you gonna pay me?"

"How much you want?"

I know Devin didn't think I was serious, but I was. Dead serious. I knew sooner or later that crazy bitch would start fuckin' wit' my dick, and my money. Either one was unacceptable. That bitch had to go. So I gave him a number. High enough that he would know I was serious, but low enough for him to think about it. "Ten grand," I said, and Devin sat up in the bed.

It worked.

I had him thinkin' about it. I cursed myself for not sayin' fifteen, but why be greedy. He turned around and looked at me. "You serious?"

"You got ten grand?"

"I could get it."

"Then I'm serious."

"Serious. You would kill my wife for ten Gs?"

"How many times you gonna ask me that? I told you, you put ten Gs in my hand, and the bitch is done."

"You ever—kill anybody before?"

"Yes."

"Who? How?"

"You don't need to know all that shit, nigga. All you need to know is that if you want me to do it, I can, and will, kill her for you," I said and rolled over.

Devin got up and went to the bathroom to take a shower. When he got out, he got dressed and came and sat on the bed.

"How would you do it?"

"You don't need to know all that either. You tell me when you want it done, and you be someplace with a lot of witnesses. I'll make it look like it was a robbery that went wrong."

Devin sat there for a while. I could tell by looking at him that he had decided in the shower that he wanted me to kill her. Now he was thinking about whether he could get away with it.

"How do I know I can trust you?"

I wasn't even about to be bothered with that shit. I sat up in the bed and moved closer to Devin.

"'Cause you gonna give me ten thousand reasons to trust me. Look, Devin, either you want me to do it or you don't. Either you trust me or you don't. It's up to you. Askin' me a bunch of fuckin' questions is just wastin' time. You go on home to your crazy-ass wife, and you think about what you wanna do. When you make up your mind, you let me know," I said and laid down. I figured I'd chill out there for the night. Maybe invite little Cutie over to finish the job that Devin started.

"I don't need to think about it." Devin stood up. "I want you to do it."

"When?"

"How soon can you do it?"

"How soon can you get me the money?"

"Tomorrow. I'll give you half; then the other half when it's done."

"You give me the money tomorrow, and I'll do it tomorrow night. But understand something. I will kill your wife, and when I do, I'm gonna want my money. No excuses. My money. Understand?"

"Yeah, I understand."

"Make sure, 'cause I won't have any problem killin' you too."

Devin smiled at me like he was tryin' to size me up.

"Don't even think 'bout that shit, nigga. I will fuckin' kill you."

"I believe you will," Devin said, and sat next to me on the bed. "Every night Taye takes sleeping pills, and after that, she is pretty much out of it. Tomorrow night I'll make sure she takes it, and that she's in bed around nine o'clock. When I'm sure she's out, I'll leave and go someplace where I can be seen. I'll leave the alarm off, you break in, kill her, take some shit, and go."

"Any cash in the house?"

"Not after tomorrow there won't be."

"Tomorrow night it is. When you bringing the money?"

"You meet me here tomorrow at one-thirty. I'll give you the money and the address," Devin said, and stood up.

"See you then," I said, and watched Devin leave the apartment.

As soon as I heard the door close, I reached for my purse. I dug around in there until I found my cell and my cigarettes. I lit up a cigarette and dialed a number.

"House of beauty, this is Cutie," she said in that sexy-ass voice.

"What's up, Cutie. This Q. What you doin'?"

"Reading a book. What about you?"

"Layin' here naked, thinkin' 'bout your sexy ass. Why don't you come by and do what you do."

I told Cutie where Devin lived, and she said she would be there in hour. I made myself comfortable and didn't think no more 'bout killin' Devin's wife. Tomorrow at one-thirty, if he handed me five Gs, I would worry 'bout it then.

Chapter Nineteen

Devin

I took one last look at Qianna before heading for the door. I left the apartment and walked toward the elevator. I was outside of the building and walking to my car, before I truly allowed myself to think. Think about what I was doing. I was talking about killing my wife—killing Taye.

On the way home, the car seemed to drive itself. One thought rolled around in my mind. I had just told Qianna that I would pay her to kill Taye.

It's not like this was the first time I'd thought about it. And each time I thought about it two things would end the discussion: one, I didn't think I could do it, and two, even if I could do it, I didn't think I could get away with it. I knew that I would be the first person that they would suspect. Spending the rest of my life in jail wasn't something I planned on doing.

The idea of getting somebody to kill her for me never entered my mind. And now that it had, now that I had told somebody, planned with somebody, agreed on a price, the question was, the only question was, did I really want Taye dead?

I thought back to my conversation with Qianna. *Serious. You would kill my wife for ten Gs?* I could hear myself saying.

How many times you gonna ask me that? I told you, you put ten Gs in my hand, and the bitch is done.

Were things that bad between us that I wanted her dead? Was I that angry with her to want her dead? Sadly, I had already answered that question. Yes, I was that unhappy with my life and the way it was going, to want her out of it.

I could just divorce her. I could go home right now, pack my things, and leave her. I could file for divorce in the morning and be done with it. I could move on with my life, and Taye could keep hers.

If I really wanted to be honest with myself, our current situation was my fault. Things really went bad for us when Taye found out that I had fucked Sandra. Since then, Taye has made my life a living hell. When I walk through the door, I never know what to expect. Since neither of her moods was good, it really didn't matter. But was it enough to want her dead for what was essentially my fault?

Sadly, the answer was yes.

What was worse was the real reason that I was even considering murder as an option over divorce, and it wasn't her mood. The real reason was money.

If I divorced her it would cost money. Since her condition is getting worse, and she refuses to take her prescribed medication, only those damn sleeping pills, she can't work at all anymore. I would be her only means of support. That meant I would have to pay all of her legal fees and court costs. I would most likely loose the house, and have to split all of our other assets, on top of having to pay her a healthy amount of alimony. The weight of all of that would be a lot for me to bear. That makes it cheaper to kill her.

But there is a flip slide to my equation. When we were first married, Taye and I took out insurance policies on each other: a million-dollar life insurance policy with a double indemnity death benefit. If Qianna killed her in what would look like a robbery, and I wasn't a suspect, I could collect that money. The truth was that I had a million reasons to want her dead.

But could I really trust Qianna? Could she kill somebody? Knowing what I know about her, which I admit isn't much, I would say, yes, she could. I've seen the knife she carries around with her all the time. *You ever–kill anybody before?*

Yes.

The question was could I trust her to do it, and keep her mouth shut? Could I trust her not to leave evidence that would lead the police to her? And if that happened, would she tell the cops everything?

I turned into my driveway and put the car in park. I got out of the car, turned on the alarm, and walked toward the house. But instead of going inside, I took a walk around the house. The floodlights came on right away. I looked at the windows and the door on the backside of the house. Then I turned around and looked at the neighbor's houses to get a feel for how visible they were.

I walked back to the front of the house and went inside, thinking that I would to turn off the floodlights before I left the house that next night. So that I wouldn't forget, I went straight to the kitchen and flipped the switch. It was located on the same panel as the back porch light. I do it accidentally all the time, anyway.

I went to the bar and made myself a drink, and sat down in my chair. Planning is one thing, but it doesn't really mean anything until I actually give Qianna the money. At this point, there was still time to back away from this. I could go upstairs, right now, and try to talk to Taye. Something I've attempted every night without success. I could tell her that I was sorry about everything that has gone on. Try to get her to see that she needed to—that we needed to recommit to some type of treatment plan.

Maybe we could find a doctor that could reach her. One that could prescribe something that she could take that wouldn't have the type of side effects that would make her like a zombie. I could tell her that we could do it together, and maybe we could reclaim some semblance of the life we once shared.

I finished my drink and went upstairs. I was determined to try. Trying was certainly better than the alternative. Certainly better than the fate I had planned for her.

When I opened the door to our bedroom, Taye was laying in bed, dressed as she usually is, in sexy lingerie. It was something that bothered me, and I never have understood. Why wear sexy lingerie if sex is nowhere in your plan?

Taye was a very beautiful woman, with a body that still, in spite of everything that has happened, makes me want her each night when I get in bed with her. It was torture for me to sleep with her every night, knowing that she won't let me touch her.

"Hello, Taye. How was your day?"

Taye looked up at me and threw the book she was reading at me. Then she got out of bed, walked over to the book, and picked it up.

"What's wrong?"

Taye got back in the bed and propped herself up. "I hate you." Then she opened the book and began reading.

I started to turn around right then, go back downstairs, fix myself a drink, and come back after her sleeping pills kicked in.

Instead, I went and sat down on the edge of the bed. I guess I got a little too close, because Taye kicked me. I moved to what I felt was a safe distance, and took a deep breath.

I spent the next half-hour trying to convince Taye that there was a better way than this. I told her that we could get through this, get through it together, and all she would have to do is say the word and recommit to treatment, and we could make it. My pleas fell on deaf ears, and after a while Taye said, "I hate you."

She turned off the light and repositioned herself in the bed. I knew there was no hope for us. I got up and went back to the bar. I sat there for the rest of the night, drinking and thinking.

Divorce or murder?

When I woke up that next morning, I was still in that chair. I got up and took a shower to get ready to go to work. When I was dressed and ready to go, I knew that it was time for me to make a decision. I stood in the doorway to my office, knowing that there was still time to change my mind.

I walked into the office and opened the safe. I had twelve thousand dollars that I had won playing poker a few months back. I took out all of it, and counted out ten thousand dollars. Then I got two envelopes, put five in one, and rest in the other.

During the drive to the work, I was surprisingly calm for somebody that was about to sanction the murder of his wife. That morning at the office was no different. I went to meetings, interacted with Winston and the rest of my co-workers, and did my job like it was just another day.

When it was time to go and meet Qianna, I left the office and drove to the apartment. She was stretched out naked on the couch watching TV, when I got there. "Hey," she said and sat up.

"How you doin'?"

"You decide what you wanna do?"

As I walked toward her, I took the envelope out of my jacket pocket.

"I guess you have."

I handed her the envelope, and she dropped it on the coffee table.

"I know I don't need to count this," Qianna said, and sat on the edge of the couch. She began unbuckling my pants. I took off my jacket and laid it on top of the money.

"No need. Five grand, like I said."

"She's done," Qianna said, and took me into her mouth.

"I'm not gonna leave the house until she goes to sleep. When I get where I'm going, I'll call you," I said, and loosened my tie. "I'll stay gone for at least four hours. That should give you plenty of time to do it." I took off my shirt and laid it on the jacket.

"Where she keep her jewelry?" Qianna asked, and took me into her mouth again.

"In the bedroom. The jewelry box is on her makeup table. I'll leave the back door unlocked when I leave."

Qianna stopped abruptly. "No. It will look better if I gotta break in. You leave all that shit to me. All you gotta do is make sure ain't no damn alarm gonna go off. When I'ma get the rest of my money?"

"Call me in a couple of days, and I'll meet you someplace."

"Why don't you just meet me here?"

"I'll let you know," I said, and looked around the apartment knowing that I would never come there again.

"Anything else?"

"No."

"Come fuck me then." Qianna bent over the couch and I fucked her.

Hard.

When I was done, I got dressed, and got back to work in time for another boring meeting. At five o'clock, Winston stopped by the office and asked me if I wanted to get a drink. We used to go out for drinks after work all the time, but that was years ago. He still asks me everyday, and everyday, I turn him down. I saw no reason to do any different. "Not today, still got a lot of work to do."

At six o'clock I left there, and took my time going home. Taye was in the kitchen, cooking herself dinner, when I got there. She made eye contact to knowledge my presence, and continued what she was doing. I took a seat at the table and began talking.

I told her again that I was sorry about everything that has gone on, and promised again that I would never let anything like that touch her. I told her that we shouldn't give up on treatment, and try to find another doctor that could reach her. Maybe they could prescribe something that she could take that could help her. I promised that we would to recommit to some type of treatment plan.

Once again, my words were met by deafening silence. When Taye finished eating, she got up from the table and went upstairs. I followed her. Taye went in the bedroom and began her nighttime ritual, while I continued to talk about getting help for her, about saving our marriage, about saving her life. That ended at eighty-thirty when Taye picked up her bottle of sleeping pills.

I sat quietly and watched her for the next thirty minutes or so; watched her until she went to sleep.

"Good-bye, Taye."

It was almost ten o'clock before I got up from the chair and went downstairs. I went to the bar in the living room, poured myself a drink, and drank it down quickly. I had another before I walked out of the house and got in my car.

I tried not to think as I drove to a pay phone to call Qianna. All I had to do to end this was not call, and it would be over. I stopped at a 7-Eleven about ten miles from the house, and pulled up in front of the phone, knowing that I had made up my mind when I left our bedroom.

I walked to the phone and dialed her number. "Hello," Qianna said.

"I'm out," I said, and hung up the phone.

I got back in the car and drove back toward the house. There was a sports bar not far from the house that Taye and I used to go to, before she lost the baby. I still go there every once and a while to have a drink and watch a game. I wasn't a regular there or anything like that, but I went there enough that the regulars knew me. I had even told Johnny, the bartender, about the problems Taye was having, one night when he asked why she didn't come with me anymore.

I went inside and waved to the people that I recognized, and took a seat at the bar. "Barcardi 151," I told Johnny when he put the napkin down in front of me.

"Comin' out the gate strong tonight," Johnny said, and went to fix my drink.

"Me and the wife are having problems again."

For the next minute or two, I caught Johnny up on what had been going on with Taye. I told him that I loved her, and didn't know what I was going to do next.

"Keep them coming," I said when he returned with my drink.

Just after Johnny put my second drink down in front of me, my cell rang. I looked at the display. It was Avonte calling. I couldn't tell you the last time I'd talked to her, much less seen her. The last few times I called her, she had some lame excuse why she couldn't get away. It didn't take me long to get the hint that she didn't want to be bothered, so I stopped calling.

Since I knew what she wanted, I started to answer the phone, but I knew that I was in the right place doing what I needed to be doing. I put the phone back in my pocket and picked up my drink.

I was pretty fucked up by the time he sat the forth one in front of me. That was also the first time that I paid any attention to the guy that had sat down next to me. He was drinking beer by the pitcher, and watching whatever baseball game was in front of him.

As the game began to go against his team, he started trying to talk to me about the game. For the most part, I just ignored what he was saying and kept on drinking. It wasn't until he grabbed and shook my arm, when his team made a big hit to tie the game that I had something to say.

Besides, I was fucked up.

"Get your fuckin' hands off me!" I yelled, and snatched my arm back.

"Did you see that? It's all tied!" he yelled back and pointed at the big screen.

"I don't give a fuck! Just don't put your hands on me again, you fuckin' asshole!" I yelled, and elbowed him.

"Who the fuck you think you talking to?"

"Talkin' to you, asshole," I said, and pushed him this time. Before I knew it, he had hit me in the face, and I fell off my chair. I got up and went right at him.

I don't remember too much after that. But I remember the bouncer coming at me, and me, taking a swing at him. I remember fighting with the police when they got there, but nothing after that, until I woke up on the floor in a cell.

Chapter Twenty

Avonte

I was alone.

For the first time since I left Tyrone, I was alone when I didn't want to be alone. Since then, anytime I wanted to play, there was somebody available to come play with me. First Devin, and then Qianna. She had been occupying all my time lately; and I've loved every second of it. But not tonight.

I haven't seen or heard from her in almost two days. I've called her several times, but she hasn't answered, so I stopped calling. I hoped that she was just busy and would call me when she could, and that she wasn't trying to give me a hint that she had moved on, and I should too. You know, the way I did Devin.

I know I could have handled it better, but I just couldn't help myself. The last few times that Devin and I were together, I thought about being with Qianna the whole time. It wasn't like I was in love with the woman or anything close to that, but I'll be damned she didn't have me so far gone on her sex, that it isn't funny. There is something about the way she grabs me by the back of my neck, and slides her tongue in my mouth, that makes me so wet. Wetter than I had ever been with either Tyrone or Devin.

I thought back to my college days with Amy. I had been dating guys before she and I got together, and became undercover lovers. But once it began, dating guys was just a front. All I wanted was Amy. I was devastated when she didn't come back to Syracuse that fall quarter. The only thing that saved me from losing my mind was the attention I was getting from Tyrone.

I knew that I had matured to the point where if Qianna was done with me that I wouldn't fall part, but right now, I was horny as hell and needed somebody to play with me.

I picked up the phone and was about to press the redial button and call Qianna again, but I dialed Devin's number instead. It had been so long since I'd called him, I had to think about what his cell number was. While the phone rang, I wondered what I would say to him after all this time. "Hey, Devin, it's Avonte. I know it's been a while since I took your call, but my clit is throbbing and I can't find Qianna. So, since you were my second choice, I decided to call and see if we could meet somewhere." When his voice mail came on, I knew he was done with me, too. I decided to leave a message anyway.

"Hey, Devin, it's Avonte. I know it's been a while since we talked, but you were on my mind. Give me a call when you get this message. Maybe we can get together some time soon. Bye."

I pressed end and rolled over in my bed. At this point, I had only two choices: get up, put some clothes on, and go find somebody and hope for the best; or I could handle the job myself. I reached in my nightstand drawer and felt around for my bullet. It had been a while since I had to use it on myself. It had become one of Qianna's favorite tools to use on me.

I put a few drop of Intrigue on the bullet and spread my legs. I closed my eyes and let my mind wander. As the sensation spread over my body, I thought about the last time I made love with Qianna and Devin.

I thought about how Qianna began running her hand across Devin's erection, and how I took his face into my hands and kissed him. Qianna stroked Devin and he unhooked her bra. As soon as her twins were free, Devin took one of Qianna's nipples into his mouth. Qianna leaned back on the couch and held Devin's head in place with one hand, and squeezed her breast with the other. I took Devin into my mouth.

In my mind's eye, I could see Qianna stand up and wiggle out of her pants. I squeezed my nipple between my thumb and forefinger, and ran the bullet across my lips.

I love the sight of Qianna's naked body. Her rich brown skin, down on her knees running her hands over my body. I love it when she takes her time and starts from my ankle, along my leg, stopping between my legs. The way she licks my lips and bites lightly on my clit always makes my river flow.

I put the bullet down, and reached between my thighs and fingered my clit with one hand, while squeezing my breast with the other. The thought and visual of Qianna and I sharing Devin came into view. I could see Qianna stroking Devin until he stood up, and she took him into her mouth. He looked down at me and Qianna running our tongues along the sides of his shaft.

I let her have the dick to herself and crawled between her

thighs. Then I very deliberately spread Qianna's lips with my thumb and forefinger, while making small circles around her clit with the tip of my right forefinger. I could feel my tongue sliding inside Qianna and sucking her moist lips gently. Feeling Qianna's body quiver as I licked her clit with the tip of my tongue. I rubbed her clit and it grew harder. Her thighs pressed together as her body convulsed. I love making her come hard like that, 'cause I know that she'll return the favor, and do me the same way.

I slid two fingers inside myself as I thought of Devin holding onto my hips, and entering me slowly, while I sucked Qianna's clit. He got into a long, rhythmic stroke, and watched Qianna squeeze her nipples in the throws of ecstasy. I came when I thought about Qianna grabbing me by the back of my neck, and forcing her tongue in my mouth. And it wasn't long before my eyes and mouth were wide open, and I was screaming my ass off. I put the bullet back in its case and drifted quietly off to sleep.

Roy Glenn

Chapter Twenty-one

Qianna

When my cell started ringing I looked over at Cutie, and she got out of bed. I looked at the display and figured that it was Devin calling.

"I'm out," he said.

"She's done," I said, and pressed end.

I'll be honest; I didn't think I'd hear from Devin that night. Even though he gave me half the money, I really didn't think that he was serious about me killin' his wife. But I guess you never know what kind of hell he was dealin' wit', and what he would do to end it. Peace of mind is a hell of a thing.

I rolled out of bed and followed Cutie into the shower. She was hard to resist, lookin' so sexy wit' the water rollin' off her skin, but we had shit to do.

Doin' the shit was one thing, doin' it and not gettin' caught and goin' to jail for it, was another. I had been down before, and I had no intention of goin' back. To me, that meant that I couldn't leave anything that would lead the cops to me. You know, DNA type shit. After Devin dropped off the money, I went out and did a little shoppin'. Our first spot was The Sports Authority on Sixth Avenue. We picked up a couple of vinyl sauna suits, some batting gloves, and ski masks, just in case Devin had it wrong, and the bitch was still awake when I got there.

My next stop was a medical supply store to get some disposable plastic shoe covers, and some plastic gloves. When we got out of the shower both of us put on our plastic gloves. From that point on, there would be no fingerprints on anything we touched. Nothing.

It was after midnight when we drove past the address Devin had given us. "Go around the block again, and park down the street where we can see the house," I told Cutie. I wanted to get a good look at things before I went inside. We had been parked about ten minutes when I saw somebody coming, and they looked like they had come from Devin's house.

As he got closer, I could see that he was a white boy with blonde hair. Either he was one of Devin's friends lookin' for him, or maybe wifey was playin' while Devin was out the house. Either way, he didn't need to see us sittin' there. "Looks like he's comin' this way," Cutie said.

"Get down," I said, and we both crouched down in our seats.

The white boy got in a sweet dark blue Benz that was parked in front of us, and drove off. We waited another half-hour after that to be sure he wasn't coming back, before we got out and moved toward the house. We put on our ski masks and put the batting gloves on over plastic gloves. I put on hers, and then Cutie put on mine.

We went around to the back door and I picked the lock. I looked at Cutie and held my breath, when I turned the doorknob. Since the alarm didn't go off, we went inside. "You have a look around, I'm goin' to look in on the Mrs.," I told Cutie, and wondered why I didn't ask Devin to draw me a little map or something.

Once I found my way to the steps, I went upstairs and found their bedroom. I opened the door slowly and peeked inside. There she was, out like a light, just like Devin said she would be. I went in and stood over her for a while. She was a very pretty woman, but I expected no less for her to be Devin's wife.

I took my time pullin' back the covers. "Damn, this bitch is fine as hell," I said softly, and she squirmed a little. It scared me for a second, until I remembered that she was just sleeping, not out cold.

I looked at her body, all dressed up in that sexy white gown. I could tell from lookin' at her, that Devin liked a certain body style in a woman, 'cause his wife was built like me and Avonte's sexy fuckin' ass.

I ran my hand along her sexy caramel skin. "Wouldn't mind havin' you myself, Sexy." Part of my plan for not getting caught was to make it look she was raped before she was murdered.

I found where Devin kept his clothes and got six of his ties. On the way back to the bed and Sexy, I saw the makeup table where Devin said she kept her jewelry. She had a lot of nice shit. Some that I wouldn't mind keepin' for myself, but that was the kind of dumb shit that would get a bitch caught and on lock down. Best if Cutie took all that shit straight to the fence.

I put the shit down for the time being, and went back to the bed. I took out my knife and a vibrator. I would push it inside her a few times, and hope that it would be enough to fool the cops. I tied her wrists and ankles to the bedposts with Devin's ties. I gagged her, then took the last one and blindfolded her.

I took a step back and looked at Sexy laying there spread eagle. I thought it seemed a little funny that her gown was gathered around her waist. I got a little closer and noticed that her panties were a little off to the side, as I cut them off her. Maybe she was masturbating before she passed out?

I cut her gown from the cleavage to the bottom, and opened it up to reveal the prettiest set of titties I'd seen in a while. When I first pushed the vibrator inside her, she squirmed and struggled a little, but after a while she seemed to relax and take it. Once I thought it had gone on long enough to leave the impression I wanted, I took it out.

"Only one thing left to do now," I said out loud, and looked at Sexy. As much shit as I talked about, I had never done nothin' like this just for money. All the others that I cut or killed deserved it.

But not her.

All she did was piss off her husband.

Then I had a rush of conscience.

Was that enough of a reason for me to kill her?

The answer was that it didn't matter. All that shit was between her and Devin. I picked up my knife and grabbed her by the chin. One quick slice and it was done. I got up from the bed and walked away as the blood eased from her wound.

On the way out of the room, I stopped at the makeup table and got her jewelry, and left her there to die.

When I got downstairs I looked around for Cutie. I found her sitting in the kitchen. "Took you long enough."

"You ready?"

"No," she said. "I need you to help me with something." While I was upstairs, she had gone through the house and had a pile of stuff sittin' by the door. In addition to lamps and paintings, there was a microwave, a nice espresso machine, a Bose acoustic wave music system, a MAC computer, and a couple of nineteen-inch TVs. "I need your help with the big screen," Cutie said, and stood up.

"How we gonna get all this shit outta here without being seen?"

"The garage is behind that door. We could back the Jeep in the garage and load up."

"Won't the light attract attention?"

"Ain't no lights on in any of the houses I can see from here. And just to be sure, I already unscrewed the bulb for the garage door, so it don't go on and stay on."

"Smart girl," I said, and kissed her.

We went and got the big screen, and then she went for the Jeep. After we had it loaded, Cutie got in and drove out of there. I closed the garage door and left the house the way I came in.

As much shit as I talk, I was glad it was done.

Chapter Twenty-two

Devin

When it came time for me to make my phone call, I called the house. If Qianna didn't do it, Taye would be up by now. The phone rang, and eventually went to voice mail. The next person I called was Winston. "Hello."

"Winston, it's Devin. Sorry to bother you so early in the morning, but I need a big favor." After I explained where I was and how I got there, Winston said he would call around and get me a bail bondsman. "Don't worry, Devin. I'll have you out of there in no time," Winston promised. By lunchtime, we were walking out of the jail toward his car.

"Thanks for putting that together for me. I really appreciate it."

"You don't have to thank me, Devin. Just be there for me next time I get drunk."

"What did you tell them at the office?"

"The truth."

"What?"

"I told them the truth. I told them that you and Taye have

been having problems, and you went out and got drunk. You had a fight at a bar, and when the police came, you fought with them too, so they locked you up."

"Couldn't you come up with anything better than that?"

"I could have," he said as we got in his car. "But they were gonna find out the truth sooner or later, anyway. Better they hear the truth from me now, than for you to have to explain the lie later."

"I guess you're right. Who you tell?"

"McNamara."

"Good choice."

"Thank you."

"What Mac say?"

"He laughed and said he'd see both of us tomorrow. So I thank you for the day off."

"Not a problem. Glad I could help you out."

"So where's your car?"

"Just take me home," I said, knowing that I wanted him to come in with me, and at least be in the house when I found the body. "I'll get my car later. Right now I just wanna go home and take a shower."

"I hear you, dude. Home it is."

When we pulled up in front of the house, I asked Winston to come in with me to have a drink.

He laughed. "No thank you. First of all, you don't need anything else to drink for a good while and two, you just want me in there to lessen the drama you're gonna get from staying out all night."

"I didn't stay out all night. I was locked up in jail all night. There's a difference."

"I used to be married. Out is out. But since I did bail you out, all I can do is to verify that I arranged bail, and then I'm out."

"Good enough," I said quickly. "Come on."

We went in the house and the first thing I noticed was that my 42-inch wide screen was gone. For some reason, I knew Qianna wouldn't be satisfied with just the jewelry.

"Something's not right," I said, and walked in the living room.

"What?"

"TV is gone," I said. "Taye, Taye. Are you here?"

I went to the garage and looked in. "Her car is still here." I began wandering around the house. "Taye, Taye!"

I stuck my head in the office and saw that she had taken my MAC and my Bose entertainment system. "I think we've been robbed."

Winston began looking around, and joined me in calling her name. "Taye, Taye!" he yelled, as I walked quickly up the steps with Winston on my heels.

I burst into the bedroom and looked at the bed. I dropped to my knees when I saw her tied to the bed in a pool of blood.

It was one thing to talk about it, plan it, but seeing her there like that, was still hard for me to take.

Winston pulled me up by my shoulders and dragged me out of the room. We walked downstairs to the kitchen, and he literally put me in a chair. My mind was racing while he picked up the phone and dialed 9-1-1.

"I'd like to report a murder and a robbery," I heard Winston say, but it still didn't seem real to me. Qianna had really done it. She killed Taye.

I got up and went outside, trying to push the image of her lying on the bed with her throat cut, out of my mind.

I made it as far as the driveway before I threw up what seemed like, every ounce of liquor that I had drank the night before.

I was still sitting outside when the police got there. Since I couldn't go back inside the house, Winston took the police inside and showed them where the body was. I sat there dumbfounded, wondering why I felt so bad about it now. Wasn't this what I wanted?

It was.

But I still couldn't move.

Maybe I was just worried about getting caught, and that's what had me feeling this way. I couldn't hide from the fact that no matter what I had done, there was still a part of me that recognized that I once loved Taye very much. And now I had killed her. So maybe what I was feeling was guilt and disgust with myself.

After a while, I don't know how long it had been, one of the detectives started coming toward me. Along the way he stopped to talk to another cop.

"You think he did it?" the cop asked.

"Not unless he could be in two places at the same time. I verified that he was in jail at the TOD," I heard the detective say. Then he approached me.

"Mr. James. My name is Detective Clinton. I am truly sorry for your loss. I know this isn't the best time, but I need to ask you some questions. Is that okay?"

I looked up at him and nodded my head.

"Your friend said that before you found the body, that you noticed that some things were missing?"

I nodded my head again.

"Can you tell me what is missing?"

"TV, computer, stereo, I don't know what else. I really didn't—I just went upstairs and I found her like that," I said, and buried my head in my hands.

"Okay, Mr. James. We can do this another time." He handed me his card. "Why don't you give me a call in a day or two."

I nodded my head and he walked away. When I looked up again, Winston was standing in front of me. "Come on, buddy, no need for you to hang around here."

"Right."

Winston held out his hand to help me up. "Can I take you somewhere? You're welcome to stay with me if you want."

"No, Winston. Thanks. Just take me to a hotel. I'll be all right." As we were walking toward his car, I stopped and looked back at the house, and thought one more time about what I had done. I got in the car and a sense of relief washed over me.

All I had to do now was get away with it.

I waited a couple of days before I called Detective Clinton back. He asked me to meet him at the house, so I could tell him what was taken. I agreed, and two hours later, we standing outside of the house, and he was going over the list of things Qianna had stolen. When we were done, he asked if I would come to the station and answer some questions for him.

When we got there, he sat me down in an office instead of the interrogation room, which to me meant that I still wasn't a suspect. But I didn't relax. I understood fully that how I answered his questions would impact my status. One suspicious answer and that all could change quickly.

Detective Clinton came back in the room with another man who he introduced as Detective Minter. After he apologized again for my loss, he got to his work.

"I know that you were arrested for disorderly conduct that

night," Minter began. "So let's start there. Why don't you tell me what happened that night?"

"I left the house about ten, ten-thirty maybe, and I went to The Sport Spot and had a few too many drinks."

"Do you usually go out drinking like that at night, or did something happen at home?" Clinton asked.

"What he's askin' is; how were things with you and your wife?" Minter asked bluntly.

"Not that good. My wife had had two miscarriages, and after the last one, she went into a manic depression," I began slowly. "Recently, she had stopped going to treatment and refused to take her medication, so her depression was getting worse."

"Why'd she stop?" Minter asked.

"She didn't like the way they made her feel."

"How was that?" Clinton needed to know.

"She said they made her feel weak and slow. She said it was hard for her to concentrate, like she couldn't focus on anything without getting confused."

"Go on, Mr. James, what happened that night?" Minter asked.

"I tried to talk to her about getting back into treatment with a new doctor, that maybe they could find something that could help her, and not make her feel that way."

"What did she say?"

"Nothing. Unless she needed to speak to me, she didn't."

"That must've been hard on you?" Clinton followed.

I didn't answer him. I just dropped my head and shook it.

"When was the last time you had sex with your wife, Mr. James?" Minter asked.

I didn't answer him either, but I looked him in the eyes.

"I know it's a very personal question, and I wouldn't ask unless it was important."

"I don't understand why, but—" I paused. "I can't tell you exactly, but I can tell you it's been a long time."

"A week? A month?" Clinton asked.

"It's been over a year now, detective."

"I see," he said.

"What happened after you tried to talk to her about treatment, Mr. James?" Minter asked.

"I went to The Sport Spot, I woke up in jail, I came home and Winston and I found her body." I dropped my head again. "You have any idea who did this?" I asked him.

"As near as we can tell, this was a robbery that went way wrong. There are signs of forced entry at the back door. The robbers came in through there, found your wife home alone."

"She takes sleeping pills at night, so she wouldn't have heard them come in."

"Yes, we found the pills by the bed," Detective Clinton said, and then he paused. "Mr. James, your wife was raped before she was murdered."

"I figured that when I saw her tied up that way," I said, and looked away.

"The good news is that we were able to get a sperm sample," Clinton said.

"What?" I interrupted quickly. "I'm sorry, what did you say?"

"Sorry, I didn't mean to say it that way, Mr. James. I mean the part about good news, I mean. There is nothing good about any of this. What I said was that we were able to get a sperm sample, and we're running that DNA against our database. Hopefully, we'll find a match."

The detectives only had a few more questions for me before they let me go. They did ask me if I would mind giving them a sample of my DNA to help with the investigation. I took that to mean to eliminate me as a suspect. "That's no problem. Anything I can do it help you catch the guy." I was glad to be getting out of there.

I drove away mad as hell with Qianna, and wondered if I hadn't made a mistake by getting her to kill Taye. I paid her to kill her. I didn't say anything about bringing some guy along to rape her before they killed her. I thought about not paying her, but that would be the worse thing I could do. Just give Qianna what we agreed on, and be done with her.

How could she be that damn stupid? If they found a DNA match to the sperm sample they had, and they caught the guy, he could turn on her. And I was sure if it came down to it that Qianna would give me up, and testify that I'd paid her to kill Taye.

So the real question was: How could I be so stupid?

Chapter Twenty-three

Avonte

I guess I've always been attracted to girls. I remember having a crush on this girl in the third grade. Back then, I didn't even know what a lesbian was. When I became a teenager and became aware of my sexual feelings, I was physically attracted to men, but I was turned on by women, too. When me and my friends were checking out the guys, I found myself checking out women too.

After my relationship with Amy began, I felt confused and unsure about whether or not I was a lesbian. I felt confused because I was still attracted to both men and women. When Amy didn't come back to school sophomore year, I started dating Tyrone, and I thought that it was just a phase I was going through, and that's all it was. But I still had those feelings. I just figured it was natural for me because of my involvement with Amy, and never gave in to those feelings. It was easy for the most part, because I never found myself in a situation where I was forced to confront those desires–until I met Qianna.

She finally called me on Friday afternoon with some excuse about leaving her cell in a friend's car, and not being able to get in touch with them to get it back until just that moment.

Whatever.

What does that have to do with her calling me?

Absolutely nothing. But I truly didn't care as long as she said she was on her way. I didn't care where she'd been for those two days. She showed up here on Friday night, and she gave this junkie her fix.

Everything was right with the world until that Monday morning, after Qianna left. On the first Monday of every month at ten o'clock, a courier comes by to drop off my money from Tyrone. Ten o'clock came, no courier. I tried not to panic though. My first thought was that it was some kind of Jewish holiday I knew nothing about, and I would have my money the next day.

No biggie; it wasn't like I was pressed for the money. When Qianna came back later that afternoon, we went out to dinner, did some shopping, and then we caught a movie. After which, we went back to my place and she ravaged my body, in ways I can't even describe.

After she finished me off, Qianna got out of bed and went in the bathroom. Before long, I heard the water running for the shower. I got up and went in the bathroom, just as she stepped in the shower. Qianna pushed the door open, and I accepted her invitation. I felt her tender lips touch mine. Nibbling softly at first; then she got rough with it, tugging on my bottom lip and holding it between hers. She grabbed my breasts and squeezed them. She used her tongue to lick around my nipples. It was driving me crazy and my juices started flowing. As Qianna bit at my nipples, she used her fingers to stroke and caress my clit. "This feels so fuckin' good!"

It didn't take long before she was kneeling down between my legs. "You taste so damn good," she pulled back to say, as she gazed into my eyes as the water rained down on her head. I spread my legs wider and she parted my lips. Her tongue flickered back and forth across my button. When I got her just where I wanted her; "Oh shit!" I screamed.

By Tuesday afternoon I was tired of waiting, so I called Albert Weinstein, Tyrone's lawyer, to see what was going on. His secretary advised me that Weinstein was in a meeting and couldn't be disturbed, but she would give him the message and have him call me. When I asked her about the money, she said she didn't know anything about it, and I would have to wait and speak with Weinstein about the matter.

Lying bitch.

Don't shit go on in that office that she doesn't know about. But instead of calling her on it, I said in my most lady-like tone, "Okay, well, thank you. I'll just wait to hear from Mr. Weinstein."

It was late on Wednesday afternoon before Weinstein finally called me back. "Good afternoon, Avonte. Sorry it took me so long to get back to you."

"It's all right, Mr. Weinstein. Thank you for getting back to me."

"What can I do for you, my dear?"

"Well," I said, and took a deep breath. "It's the first of the month, and I haven't received my check from Tyrone yet."

There was silence for a second or two before Weinstein spoke, and when he did, all he said was, "I see."

I waited to see if he was going to saying anything more. When he didn't, I did. "I was wondering if you could tell me why I haven't received it yet."

Once again, there was silence for a second or two before Weinstein answered me. "The simple answer, my dear, is that Tyrone asked me not to make anymore maintenance payments to you, until he advised me otherwise."

"What did you say?" I asked, even though I heard what he said, and was just having problems believing what he said was what I heard.

"Tyrone was in the office two weeks ago, and he instructed me to discontinue making maintenance payments to you until he gave me instructions to the contrary."

Even though I had heard him say it twice, I still couldn't believe what I was hearing. "I understand," I forced out, but I didn't. "Did he give you a reason?"

"I'm sorry, my dear, he didn't."

"Did you ask him?"

"Yes, of course I did."

"Would you mind sharing what his reason was?"

"When I asked him why he was taking this action, he said that he had his reasons, and he would speak with you about it. That's why I was somewhat surprised when you asked that question. I had assumed that by now he would have spoken with you. As I said, it was two weeks ago."

"No, Mr. Weinstein, I haven't spoken with Tyrone in months."

"I'm sorry I can't be of anymore help than that, my dear. Perhaps it would be prudent of you to speak with Tyrone."

"I guess I have no choice if I want to know what's going on, do I?"

"I'm afraid not," Weinstein said.

"Well, thank you for getting back to me, Mr. Weinstein. I'll give him a call," I said, and slammed down the phone in its cradle. *What now?* I thought as I dialed Tyrone's cell number. "Damn!" I said out loud when I heard the message saying that the number was no longer in service.

Then I called him at his office and got no answer. I left a message on his voice mail. "Tyrone, this is Avonte. Could you give me a call at your earliest convenience, please?" I said, and then I called him at the house. "Tyrone. You need to call me and explain why you told Weinstein not to give me anymore money," I said, trying to be clam about it, but I was mad as hell. Tyrone had no reason to cut me off. We had an agreement, and he was going to live up to his part of it.

I was about to call my lawyer when the phone rang. I looked at the display; it was Tyrone calling me back from his office. I tried to clam myself down before I answered. The last thing I needed or wanted was an angry conversation with him. "Hello," I said in my nicest voice.

"Hello, Avonte. I see I missed a call from you."

"Yes, you did. I just got off the phone with Weinstein, and he said that you told him to discontinue making maintenance payments to me until you gave him instructions to the contrary."

"That's right," he replied, like it was no big deal.

"Would you mind explaining to me why that is?"

"I really don't have time for this right now, Avonte."

"Well make the time, Tyrone."

"Look, why don't I give you a call later this evening. Or better yet, why don't you meet me for dinner tonight, and we can talk about it then."

"I don't think that's a good idea."

"Why not?"

"I have plans for the evening," I said to him, even though I had no plans to do anything except wait for Qianna to crawl between my thighs.

"Oh, that's right, I forgot, you're quite the socialite these days, aren't you, Avonte?"

"What are you talking about, Tyrone?"

"Like I said, Avonte, I really don't have time to go into this with you now. I'll call you later."

"Don't hang up on me, Tyrone. Why can't you just tell me what's going on?"

"Why can't you meet me tonight?"

"Because to be honest with you; I don't want to see you, Tyrone. I don't see any reason why you just can't take a minute right now, and tell me why you're doing this."

"And I don't see any reason why, if you really wanted to know, that you can't meet me."

"Tyrone," I said, knowing he could hear the absolute frustration in my voice, "you could have told me your reasoning by now. I just don't understand why we have to go through these changes, when we have an agreement."

"Yes, Avonte, we do have an agreement. And if you had taken the time to actually read the agreement, you would already know the answer to your question."

"What is that supposed to mean, Tyrone?"

"Exactly what I said. If you had bothered to read the agreement that you signed before you signed it, or at any other time since then, you would know why you won't be getting any money from me this month, or any other month."

"Tyrone, this is stupid. Why don't you just go ahead and tell me?"

"Because making you squirm is so much sweeter."

"You always could be a bastard when you wanted to."

"And you always were a dumb bitch, Avonte."

"Fuck you."

"Yeah, fuck you, too. But you still aren't getting one thin dime from me, and that makes you a dumb bitch."

"You know what—it doesn't even matter. Why don't I just have my lawyer give you a call, 'cause I don't have to sit and listen to you call me a dumb bitch. 'Cause the only dumb-bitch move I made was marrying you."

"No, Avonte. You made two dumb-bitch moves. The first was signing that prenup without reading it."

"You keep saying that, so why don't you just tell me what it says?"

"Meet me at Shooters tonight and I'll tell you."

"No, Tyrone, I already told you, I have plans."

"Yeah, I keep forgetting what a social butterfly you are. So who's it gonna be tonight?"

"What are you talking about?" I asked, but I figured that he knew I was dating, and didn't like it.

"Who's it gonna be tonight, Avonte; Devin or Qianna?"

"What?" I said, in total shock that he knew their names.

"Which one are you gonna fuck tonight? Are you gonna fuck Devin James or Qianna? Not sure what her last name is. Or if that's even her name."

"Have you been spying on me?"

"Yes. Well not me personally, but yes."

"You have no right."

"I have every right. You are still my wife."

"I don't know who your sources are, but Mr. James and I are just friends, and even if there was something between us, it is no concern of yours—especially after you and your blonde whore."

"See, Avonte, that's what makes you a dumb bitch. Who you see and what you do is my concern."

"What makes you think so?"

"Because you are still my wife; and if you had read that prenup, you'd know that by becoming involved with these individuals, you have violated the terms of the agreement, and that has the effect of making the terms of the agreement null and void," Tyrone said, laughing heartily.

"You really are a bastard, Tyrone."

"And you are such a dumb bitch, Avonte."

"Yeah, well, we'll see who the dumb bitch is after I talk to my lawyer."

"You can talk to him about anything you want. And after he reads the agreement you signed, he'll explain to you that you aren't gonna get shit from me. And then he'll tell you what a dumb bitch you are for signing it without reading it."

"Asshole!"

"Whatever. Like I said, if you want to talk about this, I'll be at Shooters later on tonight. I know I'll see you there."

"Don't hold your breath," I said with tears in my eyes, and slammed the phone down in its cradle. Now I understood why Tyrone didn't seem to be in any rush to file for the divorce. The bastard was setting me up to do this the whole time. After I called and spoke with my lawyer, and he read the agreement, I knew that Tyrone was right. I was a dumb bitch.

Chapter Twenty-four

Qianna

I gotta be honest wit' you, I always have been one dick-happy ho. You know what I'm sayin'? I'm talkin' 'bout excited to the point of tears at the sight of a big fat, juicy one. The feel of dick in my hand, in my mouth, makes my clit swell. Soft and silky when I touch it, but hard and firm inside me. I looked over my shoulder. This nigga here got a big pretty dick.

I could fuck Devin everyday, all day, the dick's so fuckin' good. Even little Cutie and the magic strap, can't compare to this nigga here. Truth was, Devin got a bitch dick-whipped, but he don't need to know all that, and I damn sure wasn't 'bout to tell him.

He spread my cheeks and slowly moved in and out of me, inchin' deeper and deeper in my ass. The deeper he got, the wetter I got. I closed my eyes and enjoyed the feeling of his stiffness inside me. The thickness of him filled me, the warmth of him inside me, long and stiff, excited me. My hips shook and I began to shake from the inside. I tried to slow my roll, but I couldn't. I felt like I was outside myself. And the feelin' only intensified the motion of my hips. When I felt him throbbing inside me, I was no longer able to control myself.

I guess you could say that we were havin' make-up sex, 'cause the nigga came up in here like he was all mad and shit. For a minute there, I really thought the mutha fucka was really 'bout to try and kick my ass. I woulda hated to kill him, good as this dick is, but I would cut his fuckin throat if he put his hands on me.

When I called him about gettin' the rest of my money, Devin started trippin'. Not about the money; about the way the shit went down. "What you talkin' 'bout? The bitch is done like I said she'd be. What's the problem?"

"You know what, Qianna, it don't even matter. I just need to meet you somewhere; and we do this and be done with it."

"That's fine with me. So you wanna meet me at the apartment in like an hour or something?"

"No. I don't think that's a good idea. Why don't you meet me at Lombardi's on Spring Street?"

"Lombardi's? What the fuck is that?"

"It's a restaurant."

"Why you wanna meet there?"

"I'm hungry."

Since I had more in mind than food, I told Devin that I wasn't feelin' all good and I didn't feel like goin' to no restaurant. It took a minute, but he finally agreed to meet me at Cutie's apartment.

When I heard the bell ring, I got out of bed, put on a black silk robe, and went to the door. I opened the door and Devin walked past me without lookin'. I smiled and closed the door.

As soon as I turned around, he tried to shove a paper bag in my hand. I walked by him without lookin', and made him follow me. I could feel his eyes on my body. He grabbed me by the arm and spun me around.

"Don't walk away from me," Devin said.

I broke loose from him and took a step back. "What the fuck is wrong with you?"

Devin threw the paper bag at me, and some of the money fell out. "Just take your damn money," he said, and turned to leave.

I grabbed his arm. "Wait a minute, Devin. You need to tell me what the fuck you so mad about." I took a step closer and put my body on him. "I did what you wanted me to do. You wanted the bitch done. I don't get what you so mad about."

Devin pushed me off him. "I paid you to kill her, not tie her to our bed and execute her!"

"I just made it look like she was raped. You know, so I wouldn't be a suspect. I wanted to make it look like a robbery gone bad."

"That's another damn thing. We talked about getting the jewelry, not my computer, my music system, and my television."

"How many times I got to say this. I made it look a robbery gone wrong, not a murder for hire. The robbery and rape shit was all part of that."

"You didn't say anything about bringing some man along to rape her!" Devin yelled, and came toward me.

"I didn't bring no man wit' me!" I yelled back. I looked around the room for my purse, but didn't see it. It's probably in the bedroom where I can't get to it quickly, if I have to. I knew he was mad, so I should have had my knife ready. "I tied her to the bed and used a vibrator on her to make it look like she was raped."

"Don't lie to me!"

"I ain't got no reason to lie to you, mutha fucka. You believe what you wanna believe," I said, and backed away from him. I started moving toward the bedroom.

"Where you going?"

"To get a cigarette," I said, and went in the bedroom. Devin followed me in and was right on top of me as I reached for it. I sat down on the bed and got the cigarettes out. Then I moved the knife so I could get to it, and set it down on the bed beside me.

I lit up, and Devin stood over me breathin' hard. "If you just used a vibrator on her, then how do you explain the cops finding semen in her?"

"What?"

"You heard me! The cops said they got a sample they collected, and they're runnin' it against their database. So don't you sit there and tell me that you didn't have some man rape her, before the two of you cut her throat."

I blew smoke in his face. "Look, Devin, you can believe me if you want to, but I don't know nothin' 'bout that shit. The only one that was wit' me was this little cutie I fuck wit' sometimes, and she was just there to help me carry the shit out. She never even went upstairs. And even if she did, she ain't got no dick."

"Then tell me what the cops got in their fuckin' rape kit?"

"I don't know, but I did see a man leavin' your house."

"What you talkin' about, Qianna? What man?"

"I'm tellin' you that when we got there, we saw a man leavin' your house. We had been parked about ten minutes when I saw somebody comin', and they looked like they had come from your house."

"What he look like?"

"White boy with blonde hair. I figured it was either one of your friends, or maybe wifey was just playin' crazy. Either way, he didn't need to see us sittin' there. I told Cutie to get down, and we both crouched down in our seats until he was gone."

"Was she awake when you killed her?"

"No."

"How long after he left did you go inside?"

"Had to be a least another half-hour before we got out and went in the house."

Devin didn't say anything. "That would still be enough time."

"Time for what?"

"If she took her pills after he left, it would still be enough time for her to be out when you got to her."

"You thinkin' she was fakin' that crazy shit, and fuckin' this white boy?"

"Yeah. That's what I'm thinking," Devin said, and dropped his head.

I stood up and tried to reach out for him. He grabbed the nape of my neck, pulled me closer, and kissed my neck. It felt as if waves of current comin' from my clit spread throughout my body. Like a greedy crack fiend, I quickly unbuckled his belt, unsnapped his pants, and reached inside his briefs. I felt its warmth then glided my hands up and down his dick. I unbuttoned his shirt; the feeling of his chest against my nipples made them swell.

He massaged my titties gently, squeezing my nipples. Devin started kissing and licking my neck, sucking and gently biting my ear lobes. Then his index finger found my clit. I reached for his shoulders to steady myself; my knees locked, my body shuddered from the inside out.

I pushed Devin down on the bed and straddled him. I grabbed hold of that dick and glided it inside me. He put his hands on my ass, and my hands dropped to his chest. I could hear him moaning quietly, his face twisted and contoured. He throbbed and I felt him expand; my fingers dug into his chest. His body became ridged; I pumped harder. His mouth was open; his eyes were locked in mine now.

After we got through fuckin', Devin got up and started gettin' dressed. I picked up the money off the floor, and put it back in the bag. "I know there's no need for me to count this."

"It's all there," he said and turned to leave.

"Before you go, I want you to know I ain't mad at you, Devin. I hate it that you mad at me. But come back and get this pussy when you calm down."

"Good-bye, Qianna." Devin turned around and walked out of the apartment. I took the money out of the bag and counted it. He was as good as his word. The money was all there.

I picked up the phone and told Cutie it was cool for her to come back. She was mad cool about the whole thing. I didn't want her having any contact with Devin. I haven't even mentioned his name to her. Cutie doesn't know that it was his house we robbed, or that while she was gatherin' up the goodies, I was upstairs killin' wifey. All she knew was that we robbed a house and got paid. The less a bitch know, the better.

When Cutie got back to the apartment, my cell started ringing. It was Avonte, and she was cryin' so much that I really couldn't make out a word she was sayin'. Cutie just looked at me and shook her head. "You got too much drama in your life for me."

I put my finger over my lips. "Calm down, Avonte, and tell

me what's wrong."

"Why don't you tell her to meet you over here, too," Cutie suggested, and sucked her teeth.

"You don't mind?"

"No, I got a date anyway," she said, and went in the bedroom.

"Avonte, listen to me. I'm at a friend's apartment. Why don't you come here, and we can talk about whatever it is that got you like this."

Avonte agreed, and I told her where Cutie lived.

I didn't see Cutie anymore until I heard the doorbell ring. I started to get up to answer, but Cutie came out of the bedroom, dressed in a short black dress that was huggin' that sexy-ass body, and said, "I'll get it."

I got a little jealous 'bout her goin' on a date, but shit, Devin was here earlier, and Avonte was at the door, so what the fuck could I say.

Cutie opened the door, and Avonte walked in. "Avonte, this is my friend Cutie."

"It's good to finally meet you, Cutie. Qianna talks about you all the time," Avonte said, while she drooled over Cutie.

"She talks about you a lot too. And Avonte . . ."

"Yes."

"You can call me Angel. Only this bitch here gets to call me Cutie. You ladies have a good night. Don't bother to wait up," Cutie said, and closed the door behind her.

"What was that about?" Avonte said, as she came to sit next to me on the couch.

"Just what she said. Her name is Angel. I'm the only bitch that get to call her Cutie."

"Oh."

There was something about the way she said "*Oh*" that I didn't like.

It was more like, "*Oh, we'll see about that.*" I knew I had to watch this bitch now.

"Tell me what you was so upset about. I could hardly understand what you was sayin' on the phone."

"I'm sorry about that. I had a chance to calm down on the cab ride over here. I'm better now."

"Well, what was wrong?"

Avonte told me some shit about her husband havin' somebody spyin' on her and shit. That he knew about her fuckin' with me and Devin, and because she signed some shit she didn't read; I don't know. Bottom line, he was cutin' her out of the money.

"That's fucked up. What you gonna do now?"

"I've got to get a job."

That wasn't what I wanted to hear. Avonte told me that she ain't never had a job in her life. "Doin' what?"

"I don't know, but I'll find something."

"What you gonna do for money?"

"I got some money saved. I'll probably have to move out of my apartment, and cut back on some things to make that money last. But I'll be all-right."

"Didn't you say that he was cheatin' on you with some blonde bitch, and that he had her all up in your house?"

"That's right."

"So how can he say that you ain't gonna get shit 'cause you doin' the same shit he doin'?"

"That's just the way it is."

"That shit ain't right." *Especially for me.*

"But he says we can talk about it if I meet him tonight at Shooters."

"What's that?"

"It's a little bar he hangs out at."

"He just wants some of that pussy."

"Don't you think I know that? I'm just not going to give him the satisfaction."

This shit is fucked up.

First Devin rolls in here all mad with me over some shit I had nothin' to do with. It wasn't my fault that he had to find out wifey was fuckin' around on him that way. But Avonte not havin' no fuckin' money, wasn't something I wasn't interested in.

We talked about it for a while longer. Then I took her in the bedroom, and gave her the comfort she came there for. Then I told her that I had some things I needed to take care of, and I would get with her later, and sent Avonte home. I had to do something to get this thing rollin' back my way.

Chapter Twenty-five

Angel

As soon as the elevator door closed, I punched the wall and regretted it right away. "Ouch." I leaned against the wall shaking my aching hand, and cursing Qianna. But what was I complaining about? I'm the one that told her to invite Avonte over. And she was kinda cute, but that's not the point. That bitch got some fuckin' nerve.

How she gonna ask me to leave my own apartment, so some man could come over to bring her money, 'cause she's too lazy to get up and go get it. And I know the nasty-bitch fucked him. I could smell it in the air as soon as I came through the door.

It is very quickly getting to the point where I can't take any more of Qianna's shit. It's like she has no conscience. It's all about what she wants, what she needs, and her desires. In spite of the fact that Qianna Patterson is by far the best lover that I've ever had, she's got to go. Just not right away.

Not before I feed this heffa a taste of what she's been feeding me lately. And I know just the man to kick things off with.

Since I had nowhere to go when Qianna put me out of my own apartment, I walked down the street to Starbucks. While I was sipping latte and nibbling on a cinnamon roll that I didn't really want, and flipping through a magazine, he called and asked me to go out with him again. Before now, my answer was always, "You know I'm with somebody. And besides you're married."

But tonight, his answer was a little different. "My status has changed," he said. So since I was mad at Qianna, I told him to meet me at The Boat Basin Cafe.

I got there early and headed straight for the bar. "What can I get for you?" the bartender asked.

"I'll have an apple martini," I said, and waited for him to get there.

I had just about finished my drink when I heard his voice.

"Hello, Angel."

"Devin?"

He smiled and shook his head. "Mind if I join you?"

It had been a good little while since we met, so as he sat down I looked him over. I met Devin one night at the club. I was there to meet Qianna, but she never showed up. And you know she had to swear up and down that she was there, and we'd just missed each other. While I was looking for her and getting madder by the second, Devin stepped to me. "Hello," he said the night we met over the music.

"Hi," I said, and continued to look around for Qianna.

He leaned close to me and said in my ear, "You're very pretty."

"Thank you," I said, and looked at Devin for the first time, and a smile creeped across my lips. I remember thinking that he was good looking, and that if I wasn't so mad at Qianna, I might have hung out with him.

"What's your name?"

"Angel," I answered in a voice that I thought screamed *I don't wanna be bothered with you.*

He stepped closer. Close enough that I could smell his cologne. "My name is Devin," he said, completely unaffected by my attitude. I looked at him again, Devin was looking and smelling good, and I was being a bitch for no good reason. *Fuck Qianna!* I said to myself, and decided right then that I wasn't going to let Qianna ruin my evening.

I held out my hand. "Nice to meet you too, Devin," I said, like my parents taught me some manners.

"Believe me, Angel, the pleasure is all mine," he said, and stared into my eyes. "I couldn't help but notice that you seem to be looking for somebody."

"Yeah. I was supposed to be meeting a friend here, but I guess she's not gonna show," I said, and looked around the club again that night. Since then, we been textin' and talkin' on the phone, but I don't remember him being this fine.

"Have a seat. I got here a little early, so I started without you. Hope you don't mind?" I said, and held up my glass.

"Not as long as you give me an opportunity to catch up." He sat down and motioned for the bartender. "Barcardi 151 on the rocks," he said, and turned to me, "Would you like another?"

"Thank you. I'll have another apple martini."

Devin and I sat at the bar and talked. Even though we had only seen each other that one time, we were very comfortable with each other. I liked talking to Devin. His conversation was always so positive, and filled with ideas that opened my mind to new possibilities. He was a refreshing change from Qianna.

"Mind if I ask you a question?"

"Go ahead."

"Every time I asked you to go out with me before, you always said no. Why did you say yes today?"

I smiled at him for a second or two before I answered his question. "The politically correct answer would be that I just wanted to see you. But the truth is a bit more complicated."

"You feel like sharing?" Devin asked, and moved a little closer to me.

"I'm mad at my friend, so here I am."

"What did your friend do to make you mad?"

"Oh nothing; just seeing two other people."

"Damn. I'm sorry."

"Don't be," I said, and raised my glass. "It's my fault. I let this happen. So I have nobody to blame but myself. You try to be understanding. You know, give people their space and let them be who they are, do want they gotta do to make it. But damn, show me some respect."

"Nobody likes to be disrespected."

"I knew they were seeing other people, but so am I, so that's not the problem. Then they started bringing them to my apartment when I wasn't there."

"That's just wrong."

"I think so. But let me ask you a question."

"What's that?"

"Would you bring your other woman, not saying that you got another woman, but would you bring her to your house to have sex with her?"

"No."

"Even if your wife said it was all right?"

"No."

"Why not?"

"That would be too disrespectful."

"That's exactly my point, and I'm getting tried of it."

"You shouldn't have to put up with that."

"It's gotten to the point where they don't even try to hide it anymore. It's like she doesn't care about my feelings."

"She?"

"She," I said, and looked Devin in the eye, and waited to see his reaction.

"You are–" he started, but I saved him the trouble.

"Let's just say I like people."

"I see."

"I don't like labels, so I don't apply them to myself. That way, I don't apply them to other people."

"Very enlightened attitude."

"Does that bother you?"

"Does what bother me?"

"You know what I mean," I said, and took a playful swing at him. "Does it bother you that I like having sex with women?"

"No. Not at all. This may come as some surprise to you, but I like having sex with women too. So no, it doesn't bother me at all. That is, as long as you like having sex with men, too."

"Yes, I like having sex with men too. And why do you care? You should only be interested in having sex with one woman, and that's your wife."

"My wife died recently."

"I'm sorry, I didn't know."

"I don't like talking about it."

"I understand completely. We'll talk about something else."

"The subject we were on was fine with me."

"What; me liking sex with men too?"

"Yeah that."

I smiled and sipped my drink. "What about it?"

"Do you have a preference for one gender over another?"

"Not really. I don't deny my attraction for one over the other."

"Most of the bisexual women I've met, say they prefer women over men. They say that a woman knows what a woman wants."

"I've met quite a few women that have told me that too. But I try to focus my attractions on qualities I see in an individual, regardless of whether that person is a man or a woman. Sometimes these qualities involve gender, sometimes they don't."

"Like what?"

"I may be attracted to the fullness of a woman's hips or her breasts. Or I may look at a man's hands and feet, or the way he walks, and become intrigued by the size of his tool, for lack of a delicate description."

"Is that a fact?" I asked, and smiled confidently.

"Usually. Big hands, big feet, big tool."

"I wear a size thirteen."

"I noticed," I said, then reached over and touched his hand. "And your hands are pretty big, so I was intrigued."

"How intrigued are you?"

"Intrigued enough to wanna have sex with you tonight."

Devin stood up and signaled for the bartender. "Check, please." He paid the check, and I followed him to a hotel. A very nice hotel; and it was only a few blocks away. I assumed that he wasn't trying to go too far, and run the risk of me sobering up and backing down. There was no chance of that happening. "I'm fuckin' you tonight."

Once we got to the room, he tried to kiss me right away. "Slow down," I said, and gently pushed him off of me. "We got plenty of time for all that."

Devin sat down on the edge of the bed. I unzipped my dress and allowed it to fall to the floor. I stood in front of Devin in only my bra and thong.

"Stand up," I said, and then I undressed him. Kissing and teasing him as I took off each piece.

When he was naked, I sat on the edge of the bed. Devin knelt down on the floor and slowly eased my legs apart. He began massaging my calves, and did the same to my thighs. Devin peeled off my thong and began exploring my moist lips with his tongue, until he made my body shake.

I sat up on the bed. "Lie down on your back; let me do you."

Without a word, Devin smiled and quickly complied with my request. I knelt on the bed next to him, and tried to remember the last time I sucked a man's dick. It had been a minute, but I was sure it would come back to me. I ran my tongue across his nipples and slowly worked my way down to his dick, and thought for a second about Qianna. I took Devin all in, and all I could hear was Qianna saying, "That's it, Cutie, gag on the cock," as she eased the dildo deeper in my mouth.

Chapter Twenty-six

Devin

It seemed as though Angel's touch made my head spin. I felt a rush of warmth while she sucked my dick. It felt like it was all happening in slow motion.

Angel straddled me as I looked on with great anticipation. She slid down on me. Angel moved slowly up and down, then in circles. She leaned forward and kissed me. I could taste the apple martini's she'd been drinking as her tongue moved over mine. Angel moved from side to side, rubbing her chest across mine, in beat with the music. The sensation I felt when I felt her nipples rub against mine, sent chills over my whole body. I ran my hands down her back and across her cheeks, as she started to move her hips faster. Her skin was so soft.

Then Angel sat up and went to work. After a while, she stopped and moved her legs so her feet were on the bed. Then she proceeded to fuck the shit out of me. Then she hopped off quickly and took me into her mouth again, while she fingered herself.

"Come sit on the edge of the bed," Angel commanded, and stood up.

I quickly inched to the edge of the bed. Angel turned around and straddled me. She took my dick in her hand and eased herself down on me. Then she put her hands on my chest to steady herself.

I grabbed Angel by her wide hips and pushed myself inside her. I sat up and ran my hands over her upper body. I took one of her titties in my hand. I had never felt anything so soft. I squeezed her nipple while I massaged her clit with the other.

She put her feet on my thighs and proceeded to ram her body into mine. After that, Angel got up and began to get dressed. "Get up, Devin, I gotta go."

I looked at the clock: 12:45 AM. I shrugged my shoulders and got up. I got dressed and we left the room. Angel told me where she wanted to be dropped off, and we drove there in silence.

We arrived at her spot. As soon as I put the car in park, Angel leaned over and kissed me on the cheek. "Good night, Devin. I had a good time tonight." She kissed me on the cheek again, and practically jumped out the car.

"Angel," I said, and she stuck her head back in the car. "Can I see you again?"

"I'll call you." Then Angel closed the car door and walked quickly toward the building. I knew then that she was just grudge fuckin' to get back at her girlfriend. But the pussy was good, so I ain't sayin' nothing.

Chapter Twenty-seven

Avonte

If there is one constant in the world, it's that nothing lasts forever. After melting down with Qianna, and spending the night on the phone crying with my parent's, I came to one very important conclusion. I refuse to let this keep me down.

I got up early that next morning and began the process of planning the rest of my life. I logged on to my bank's Web site, and checked the balances on my accounts. Once I had an idea of where I stood financially, I did a budget. As much as I didn't want to, I knew that I would have to move to something a little less pricey, if I was going to make that money last.

The first thing on my agenda was to find a job. Something I had never done before. Not even as a teenager. There was no after-school job at a fast food joint for me. I thought I was too cute for the burger girl uniform.

The only work I had actually done was volunteer work for the charitable organizations that Tyrone and I gave money to.

Thinking that they would be a good place to start, I decided to make a few calls and do a little networking.

What I found brought the reality of my situation clearly into focus, but was not entirely surprising. Each of the people I called, people that I once considered friends, none of them offered any help. In fact, their tone was decidedly cold toward me. It made me realize that the only reason that I was accepted in those circles was because I was Tyrone's wife. Now I had reverted back to what I always was in their eyes.

The nigger-bitch Tyrone married.

Determined not to let any of that get the best of me, my next stop on-line was monster.com. Since I never had a job, there was nothing to put on a resume. I decided that I would do some research on the site to see if they had any advise to offer.

I read articles on turning your job interviews into job offers. Opening doors with a high-impact resume. There was one on using a resume writing services to give me the resume that promised to get me the job at every level of my career. I read about how to determine my value, how to protect myself from being underpaid. I laughed when I came upon an article called "Networking 101" that told me that it'll take more than small talk and business cards to connect with others. I had already tried networking with the people I knew, and that got me nowhere.

I had just finished reading an article titled "Is Now the Time to Get into Real Estate Sales", when the doorbell rang. I checked the time; it was just after three in the afternoon. I went to answer the door thinking that it was too early for Qianna to show up here, and wondering who else it could be. There weren't a lot of people that knew where I lived.

When they pressed the bell again, I asked, "Who is it?" I peeked out the hole and saw two cops standing there.

"Police, ma'am. We're looking for Avonte Petrocelli."

I opened the door. "I'm Avonte Petrocelli. Is their some problem?"

"Mrs. Petrocelli, I'm sorry to have to tell you this, but your husband Tyrone Petrocelli is dead."

"What?"

"You have our deepest sympathy," the other said.

Tears began to roll from my eyes. "Oh my God, how? When?"

"His body was discovered this morning by the housekeeper."

"Did Carmen say what happened? Was there some type of accident?"

"No, ma'am; there was no accident. Your husband was murdered. Would you mind coming with us to identify the body?"

"No, no, of course not. Just give me a minute to change."

"That's not necessary," the officer said.

"Oh—okay. I'll get my purse," I said, and left with the police. On the way to the station all kind of things rolled through my mind. First I had to decide how I felt about it. That wasn't hard. What he did to me was wrong, but nobody deserves to die. Then I wondered who could have killed him. Did somebody break-in the house to rob it? Maybe Tyrone surprised them and they killed him.

Knowing that he could be an asshole sometimes, the possibility exists that he may have pissed somebody off enough to kill him. Or maybe it was his new blonde bitch.

"Do you know how he was killed?" I asked the officer.

"No ma'am."

"We're just taxi service," the other officer said, and laughed.

After a long ride from Manhattan, we finally arrived at The

City of Glen Cove Police Department headquarters, on Bridge Street in beautiful downtown Glen Cove.

When we got there I was met by a very attractive detective. "Mrs. Petrocelli, my name is Detective Jensen," she said, and offered her hand. "I'm very sorry for your loss. If you could come with me, we'd like you to identify the body."

I went with the detective, and before too long, we were standing over the body. I felt a rush of cold all over my body. Before all this began, I had come to love Tyrone very much, and the idea that he was murdered and I was there to identify him, shot through me.

When Detective Jensen pulled back the cover, I looked at Tyrone. All the color was gone from his face. I looked away and shook my head. "Thank you, Mrs. Petrocelli," Jensen said, and pulled the cover back over his face.

Thinking that we were done, I started to walk away, but Jensen stopped me. "I'm sorry, Mrs. Petrocelli." Jensen turned to the table next to the one Tyrone was on. "But would you mind taking a look at this body?"

Jensen pulled back the cover and I looked at the woman on the table. She was a white woman with long blonde hair. At first, I thought it could be the bitch he left me for, so I took a closer look. "Do you know her?"

"No," I said, and looked again. "I've never seen her before."

"Are you sure?"

"Yes, I'm sure. I've never seen her before."

"Thank you." Jensen covered the woman's body and asked me if I would mind coming with her. "I have a few questions that I'd like to ask you."

When we got to her office she offered me a seat. "Once again, Mrs. Petrocelli, I'm sorry for your loss."

"Thank you," I said, more because I didn't know what else to say. "Could you tell me what happened?"

Jensen opened her notes. "Your husband's housekeeper, a Carmen Wilson, found the body when she came to work this morning. He had been stabbed in the chest with a kitchen knife." Jensen pushed a picture of the body in front of me. Tyrone was lying on the kitchen floor in a pool of blood. The knife was still lodged in his chest.

"You and your husband are separated, is that correct?"

"Yes, that's right."

"And you maintain a separate residence in Manhattan, is that correct?"

"Yes."

"How long?"

"About eight months now."

"Your idea; his idea?"

"His. My husband began seeing another woman and told me he was filing for divorce. I moved out after that."

"How were things between the two of you since then?"

"We really hadn't spoken much since then. For the most part, we communicate through our lawyers."

"I know that must have been tough on you."

"It was. You don't know what hurt is until you come home and find another woman in your house."

"I read the report."

"You did?"

"Yes." Jensen flipped a few more pages. "She thought you broke in, and called the police on you. She must have looked pretty foolish when the officers told her that you were his wife, and she had to leave."

I laughed a little when I thought about it. "She did look pretty stupid."

"It says here that you hit her."

"To be honest with you, I knew who she was, and I knew I wouldn't get another chance, so I tried to slap the taste out of her mouth."

Jensen laughed. "I wish I could have done that to the bitch my prick husband left me for."

"Every woman's dream."

"And you say that was eight months ago. When was the last time you spoke with Mr. Petrocelli?"

"Yesterday afternoon."

"What did you talk about?"

It was only when she asked me that question, and I thought about the fact that we argued because he had cut me off from the money, did I realize that I could be a suspect in his murder. "We talked about the divorce," I said, without going into any more detail.

"How's that going?"

"The divorce?"

"Yes."

"The lawyers were working out the details."

"But you did talk to him yesterday. Did you see him?"

"No, we spoke by phone."

"So you didn't go to the house?"

"No. I haven't gone there since that day I caught her there

and I moved out."

"You mind telling me where you were last night about eleven-thirty?"

"I was at home."

"Were you alone?"

"Yes."

"Can anybody verify that?"

"No, not really."

"What were you doing?"

"I was on the phone talking to my Mom and Dad most of the night, and then I went to bed."

"What time was that?"

"That I went to bed; or that I was talking to my parents?"

"Both."

"I called them about nine, and we talked for a couple of hours, I guess. Then I went to bed."

"About what time was that?"

"It was some time after eleven. Am I a suspect, detective?"

"To be honest with you, Mrs. Petrocelli," Jensen said, and then she paused. "I'm just trying to rule you out."

"Can you tell me what happened?"

"Of course we're still investigating, but we think your husband's murder was a crime of passion."

"What do you mean by that?"

"When the body was discovered by the housekeeper, Mr. Petrocelli was naked on the kitchen floor. The woman I asked you if you knew . . ."

"Yes."

"She was naked too. The housekeeper found her in the living room with her throat cut."

"Oh my God."

"We think that the killer came in and found them having sex, and killed them both."

"And you think I did that?"

"Like I said, Mrs. Petrocelli, I'm just asking questions; trying to eliminate you as a suspect. About the woman I asked if you could identify."

"Yes."

"Was that the woman you saw that day at your house?"

"No, it wasn't."

"Are you sure? I only ask because of the way you were looking at her."

"At first, I wondered if it was. I had only seen her the one time, so I took a second look to be sure that it wasn't her."

"And you're sure?"

"Yes, detective, I'm sure. What happens now?"

"Well, right now, I'm going to check out your story. If what you told me is the truth, that you were home last night and on the phone, you'll be free to go."

"I understand. I assure you, detective; I had nothing to do with any of this."

Jensen pushed a pen and paper at me. "Would you mind writing down your parent's names, and their number for me?"

I wrote down the information she requested, and handed it back to her. "I promise it won't take long to verify what you told me," she said, and left me alone in her office. Left me thinking who could have done this to Tyrone, and hoping that it wouldn't touch me.

Chapter Twenty-eight

Qianna

Okay, things didn't go like I planned with Avonte's husband. I swear 'fore God that I didn't plan on killing him. The only thing I wanted to do was make shit even. It wasn't right for him to be fuckin' around on Avonte, but when she does the same shit, he cuts her off from the money. That shit ain't right.

So, my plan was simple. After Avonte told me where he wanted her to meet him, I went out there. Avonte had shown me a picture of him, so I knew him as soon as I saw him. When I got there, he was standing at the bar, talking with some little blonde cutie. I watched them for a while, thinking about how I was gonna get to him, when she pulled out a cigarette. I got up from my spot and followed her outside.

"Can I get a light from you?" I asked.

"No problem. We smokers have got to stick together, you know," she said, and handed me her lighter. "Pretty soon they'll be telling us that we can't even smoke in our own houses."

"I know that's right." I took a drag off my cigarette, and gave her back her lighter. "That's how the system works, honey. Government got to be in control of every part of your life."

We talked while we smoked our cigarettes. Funny how smokers can always find something to talk about. "I'm Iris," I lied and smiled.

"Laurie. Nice to meet you, Iris."

"That's a very nice outline you have on," I said, even though it wasn't. The shit looked like she bought it at Kmart.

"Thank you," Laurie said, and smiled.

"It suits you. You're very pretty too," I said, and Laurie blushed. By the time we finished our cigarettes and went back inside, Laurie and me were like the best of friends. It always has cracked me up how some bitches will tell a complete stranger all their business over a cigarette. Laurie was one of them bitches.

Laurie told me she was from Kansas. "I had to get away from Jeff; that was my boyfriend. He was one crazy mother fucker." She told me how her boyfriend used to beat her, and about her drug and alcohol issues. "I got it under control now. But for a while there, I thought I was gonna die." And then she told me that her tits were fake. She even let me feel them. "Go ahead, I don't mind." Them shits was hard as rocks.

"Go ahead, feel mine. I don't mind," I said. Laurie giggled, but it didn't take long before she was smiling and squeezing.

When we got back inside, we went to the bar to join Tyrone at the bar. Laurie introduced us. "Tyrone, this is my friend Iris."

Judging by the way that his eyes bulged out of his head when he turned and looked at me, I knew I could get him to go with me.

The only question now was whether I was going to bring Laurie along for the fun.

Tyrone ordered a round of drinks, and the three of us talked. I told them that I was there to meet somebody, but they hadn't gotten there yet. But I made it obvious that I was down for whatever.

After a lot of me flirting with the two of them, plenty of sexual innuendo and three more drinks, Tyrone and Laurie were ready to go and take their thing to the next level. "We're gonna head to my place, keep this party going. Why don't you come with us?"

"What's happenin' at your place?" I asked innocently.

Tyrone leaned closer. "Have some drinks, do a few lines," he said in my ear. "Then, you know, whatever."

I looked at Laurie and then back to Tyrone. "Yeah, whatever sounds good," I told them, and we left the bar.

It didn't take long to get to the house. When we pulled up in front of the house, I was shocked by how fuckin' big the place was. Tyrone was ballin' for real. I see why Avonte was trippin' about losin' this money.

Shit, I see why I was trippin'.

All it took was a glass of wine and a few of lines of coke, before Laurie came outta her Kmart dress and was paradin' around in her pumps and panties.

When Tyrone took off his clothes, and they both started encouraging me to get comfortable, I knew it was time for the next part of my plan. I was gonna get this whole set on camera.

Me and Avonte were out shoppin' one day, Avonte loves to shop, but that day I told her that I wanted to get a digital camera so I could take pictures of her. Maybe even make a movie of us fuckin'. So Avonte bought me a Sony Cybershot 10 megapixel digital camera.

I got up and looked around the room for a good spot to setup the camera. There was a credenza over by the staircase that was the perfect height, and wasn't too far away. While I got naked I set the camera on the table, and put my clothes around it for cover.

"What are you doing over there?" Tyrone asked and started coming toward me.

"Nothin'. Just gettin' comfortable."

"What's that you got there?" He pushed me out of the way and knocked the clothes off the camera. It didn't take him long to figure out what the camera was for.

Tyrone grabbed me and demanded to know who I was, and who sent me. "Avonte sent you, didn't she? You're the bitch she's fucking, aren't you?" he started shaking me.

"I don't know who you talkin' 'bout! Take your mutha fuckin' hands off me!" I yelled, and tried to get free.

"Who sent you?"

Tyrone reached back and slapped the fuck outta me. He hit me so hard that I fell to the floor. I got up and tried to run, but he grabbed me and hit me again. I swung at him and scratched his face. "You fucking bitch."

Tyrone came at me and I ran. While Tyrone chased me around the living room, that bitch Laurie, sipped her drink and did another line.

I ran into the kitchen looking for something to throw at him. I picked up the bottle of wine we were drinking, and threw it at him, but I missed and he kept comin'. Then I threw a frying pan at him, but he ducked. The only thing that saved me was that he was off balance when he did that. He slipped on the wine and hit the floor hard.

I grabbed a knife from the counter and dove on top of him. I pushed the knife into his chest as hard as I could. "I got your bitch."

I went back into the living room. Laurie was still powdering her nose, like nothin' else was goin' on around her. I went to the credenza and got my knife from my purse.

"Where's Tyrone?" Laurie asked when she finally looked up.

"He's on the floor in the kitchen," I said, and walked around behind her.

"What's he doing on the floor?" her dumb-ass asked, and laughed a little.

"Waitin' for you." I grabbed a handful of her hair, and slid my blade across her throat.

I got dressed as fast as I could, and looked around the house to see if I could find whatever he had on Avonte. I found what I was looking for on the desk in his office.

It was in a large manila envelope, and it had a lot of pictures of Avonte with me, and then there were two shots of her and Devin having dinner at some restaurant. There was also a written report of the places that Avonte and I had gone together, and the same for Devin.

Whoever made this report knew everything about Devin, but they didn't know much about me, other than my first name. All they had on me was bad pictures of us eating, shopping, and getting in and out of her car. I took the envelope and got outta there.

Then I wiped down everything that I thought I might have touched. Then I thought about the bottle of wine I threw at Tyrone. If the cops got even a partial print off a piece of that broken glass, I'd be fucked. I went in the kitchen and picked up every piece I could find, and then got a broom to sweep up.

I left there walking, and called a cab to pick me up at the first place I got to. From there, I got a room at a motel and laid low for a couple of days; and hoped I had dodged another bid.

After a couple of days in that room, I was gettin' bored and lonely. I needed to get out, see some people, maybe even get some dick.

And if I was gonna try and get some dick, I might as well try to get with Devin. I knew if I called him, he would probably hang up on me. So, I caught a cab and went to a bar that wasn't too far from where he worked, to see if he was there.

When I got there, the first person I saw was Devin. He was at a table close to the bar talking to some white guy. I had started walking toward them when I got the feeling that I knew the white boy he was with. I stopped dead in my tracks when I realized that he was the white boy that I saw that night, coming out of Devin's house.

I couldn't be sure if he saw me and Cutie that night, and I was in no mood to find out. The last thing I needed was for him to recognize me. I started to go to the bar, but when I turned to walk away, I heard Devin call me.

"Shit."

I turned around and Devin was waving me over to their table.

"Shit," I mumbled, and went to the table.

Both men stood up when I got to the table. "What are you doing here, Qianna?"

"Maybe I was lookin' for you."

"Winston, this is my friend Qianna," Devin said, and I waved to him.

"Nice to meet you, Qianna," Winston said, and we all sat down. It didn't seem like the white boy recognized me. I wondered if Devin even suspected that this boy was fuckin' his wife.

"Can I talk to you for a minute, Devin?"

"Sure. I was just getting ready get out of here anyway. Winston, I'll see you in the morning."

"Not if I see you first," Winston said, and laughed. Neither me nor Devin got the joke, and we walked away.

Once we were far enough from the table, I turned to Devin. "You remember I told you that I saw a white boy comin' out of your house that night?"

"Yeah, what about it?"

"That's him."

"Winston? Are you sure?"

"Does he drive a sweet dark blue Benz?"

Devin looked at me. "He does."

"Then I'm sure that's the same guy."

"Damn. He always did have a thing for Taye. I can't believe he was fuckin' her." Devin started to go back to the table, but I stopped him.

"Where you goin'?"

"Where you think I'm goin'?"

"No, there's a better way to deal with him."

"How's that?"

"He was fuckin' her, right?"

"Right."

"Cops told you they had DNA and were lookin' to find a match, right?"

"Yeah, you're right, they do."

"You go on and get outta here. I'll make sure he's our guy."

I stood and watched Devin until he left the bar, before I went and joined Winston at the table. "Hi."

"Welcome back," he said, and looked surprised when I sat

down next to him. "I thought since you came here looking for Devin, that you were leaving too."

"No, I'm lookin' for somebody to play with me." I ran my hand slowly across his face. "You wanna play with me?"

"Yes," Winston said quickly, and started trying to flag down his waitress to get the check. "I don't live too far from here."

While he waited for his waitress, I told him that I was going to the ladies room, and that I would meet him outside.

When he came out, we went to his car and he drove me to his apartment. The minute we made it to the bedroom, this mutha fucka was all over me. I pushed him off of me and he fell on the bed. He sat there quietly with a big smile on his face, while I took off my clothes. "Now stand up," I demanded, and he did what I asked. "Take off your clothes."

Chapter Twenty-nine

Winston

She didn't have to tell me twice. I started pulling off clothes so fast that she started laughing. She could laugh all she wanted, as long as she gave me some of that pussy. Qianna was fine as hell. I would have to thank Devin for this one in the morning.

Fact of the matter was that I owed Devin for more than just walking away and leaving me with Qianna, but for being such an asshole and leaving Taye at home alone every night.

It all started simple. I was in their neighborhood one night, and I decided that I would drop by to say hello. I pulled up in front of the house, but I didn't see Devin's car in the driveway. That didn't matter to me one way or the other. He could be parked in the garage or not even home. Either way, I was there to see Taye anyway.

I've been in love with Taye since the first time I met her. It was at the company Christmas party, and naturally, Taye came with Devin. She was dressed in a flowing white gown that highlighted her shoulders.

"Winston, this is my wife, Taye," Devin said that night at the party.

"Well, it is nice to finally meet you, Winston," Taye said, and took my hand in hers. "Devin talks about you all the time."

Her hands were warm, and Taye had the most beautiful smile. And the deepest brown eyes that seemed to look inside me, and reach my soul. "I hope it was good," was all that I could manage, as Taye smiled at me and continued to hold my hand.

"You know I had nothing but good things to say about you, buddy," Devin said to interrupt the trance Taye had me caught up in.

"Oh yes, Devin speaks very highly of you," Taye said, and finally let go of my hand.

"That's good to know," I said, and let out a goofy giggle. I felt like such a fool.

"Well, it was nice meeting you, Winston. I'm sure I'll see you again," Taye said graciously, and went off with her husband; taking my heart with her.

Over the years the three of us got together pretty regularly. Taye would come and have drinks with us after work. During those times, Taye and I became friends, but I never told her how I felt about her. That would have been inappropriate. I was just happy to be in her presence, and happy with the guy friend hugs and kisses on the cheek, that she gave me each and every time she saw me, and wished there was something more.

Then she lost the baby.

I went to see Taye in the hospital. She was asleep when I got there. I stood there staring at her, and I held her hand. I touched her face and I felt the strongest urge to kiss her.

I leaned forward slowly and was about to kiss her when Devin, who always did have the worst timing, walked in the room.

"Hey, Babe," he said as he burst through the door carrying a dozen roses. I let go of her hand and straightened up quickly. If Devin saw me, or had any idea what I was about to do, he never said anything about it. Taye opened her beautiful eyes and smiled at me, smiled like she knew that I loved her, and then turned to her husband. I didn't see much of Taye after that, and hadn't seen her at all since they she lost their second child.

I went to the door and rang the bell. There were lights on in the house, but know one came to the door. I rang the bell and waited.

The truth is that I knew Devin wasn't there, and I didn't just happen to be in the area. I knew Devin was out with whoever he was seeing. I was passing by his office and heard him making plans to meet her.

Taye had been through enough, and shouldn't have to deal with her husband being unfaithful to her. She deserved a man who would be patient with her, and be understanding of what she's going through.

A man like me.

I would break it to her gently, and then be there to comfort her through her tears. Offer her support throughout the divorce proceedings. And when it was all over, Taye would turn to me, because by then, she'll know that I love her.

How did things get so far away from there?

Why didn't I just leave when nobody answered the door after

the second ring?

I knocked on the door and was about to leave when I glanced back, and saw Taye come down the steps.

I should have known that something was wrong, when she walked past the door without opening it. I rang the bell again, and banged on the door; all the while, calling her name. "Taye!"

Not only didn't she come to the door, Taye didn't even look back. I stood there ringing the bell, over and over until I saw her coming. But instead of coming to open the door, Taye headed back toward the steps.

"Taye!" I screamed at the top of my lungs, and she turned toward the door.

Finally, she came to the door and turned on the porch light. "Who is it?"

"Taye, it's Winston," I said, and she opened the door.

"Devin's not here," she said, and held the door.

She was wearing a white silk robe, and a white gown with spaghetti straps that barely covered her. I knew something wasn't right when she didn't try to cover herself. We stood there staring at one another until I finally said, "Can I come in–and use your bathroom?"

"I'm sorry. Come in," Taye said, and stepped aside to let me in.

"Thanks," I said, and walked past her slowly. "I know where it is." Instead of thinking that something wasn't right, and that I should leave, my mind went in a totally different direction. All I could think about was how sexy she looked, and how much I wanted her. How much I've always wanted her. Instead of thinking that something wasn't right, I imagined that Taye hadn't bothered to cover herself because she wanted me the way I wanted her. I stayed in the bathroom for a couple of minutes before I came out.

When I went back to the door, Taye was sitting in the living room with her eyes closed. I sat down across from her and then I called her name, and Taye opened her eyes.

I just started talking, but it wasn't long before her eyes drifted shut. "Taye," I said, and stood up. I walked over to her and touched her gently. "Taye, are you all right?" When she didn't answer, I touched her neck to see if she had a pulse. It was then that I remembered Devin mentioning that Taye took sleeping pills some times.

Now that I knew she was just sleeping, I picked her up and carried her upstairs to their bedroom. I laid her down on the bed, and stood over her to admire her beauty. I should have left then.

But I didn't.

I sat down on the edge of the bed and I kissed her. Kissed her lips the way I had always wanted to, for all these years. She didn't wake up.

I ran my hand along her cheek, down to her neck, and across her chest. I felt her breasts with one hand and then the other. She didn't wake up.

I pulled up her gown and stuck my fingers in my mouth. With my index finger, I massaged her clit and looked at her face. She squirmed a little when I slide my fingers inside her, but she didn't wake up.

I unbuckled my pants and pulled down my zipper. I started to stroke myself while I slid my fingers in and out of Taye. She was so wet. I left after I came in my hand.

The next morning, I went into Devin's office, just like I did every morning. I needed to know if Taye had even mentioned that I had been to their house the night before, but he never said anything about it.

After that, I couldn't get Taye out of my mind. I had to have her again. I went back to their house one night the following week. I knocked on the door, I rang the bell, I called her name, but she didn't come to the door. I left disappointed, but determined to have her. No matter how wrong it was, I had to be inside Taye.

That next day at the office, I stuck my head in Devin's office. "Let me see your keys, buddy. My battery's dead, and I need to run out for a minute."

"You need help?" Devin said, and dug in his pocket for his keys.

"I'll jump it off when I get back; if that's all right with you, of course?" I asked, and Devin threw me his keys.

"Not a problem."

"I'll even put gas in it," I said, and went to the nearest locksmith, and got a copy of their house key.

That first night, I felt apprehensive as I unlocked the door and hoped that the alarm wasn't on. My heart was pounding in my chest when I stood in the bedroom door, and looked at her lying there, sleeping so beautifully, waiting for me to have her.

Chapter Thirty

Qianna

Winston began frantically pulling the clothes from his body. When he was naked and standing in front of me, I had to bite my lip to keep from laughin', 'cause his dick was so small. "Lay down on the bed," I instructed, and picked up his belt and tie.

"What are you gonna do?" Winston asked, but he got his ass on that bed.

"I'm gonna fuck the shit outta you," I promised, and crawled on top of him. I thought about suckin' his little pink dick, but what would be the point in that. I used his tie and belt to tie him to the bed. Then I got up and got his shirt. I ripped it, and used the pieces to tie up his legs.

Now that I had him spread eagle on the bed, I got my purse and took out my knife.

"What you gonna do with that knife?" he needed to know when I came and sat on the bed.

"It's to make sure that you're a good boy, and give me what I want." I ran my hand up and down his little dick a few times, and that seemed to satisfy his need to know as I got on top of him.

"Oh, I promise to be good, baby. I'm gonna give you everything you want."

"You promise?" I asked softly, and slid myself down on his little dick.

"Anything," he promised, and began to move. I rode him for a while just to see how, or I should say if, I could feel him, and then I rolled off. "What's wrong? Why'd you stop?"

I moved the knife along his leg and close to his dick. I grabbed it by the head, and held the knife to it. "You were fuckin' Devin's wife, weren't you, white boy?"

"I don't know what you're talkin' about," he protested. "Be careful with that thing."

"Don't lie to me. You were fuckin' Devin's wife, weren't you?"

"I think this has gone on long enough. I think you need to untie me right now."

"I don't think so."

I took my knife and made a small cut on the head of his dick. "Ouch!" he screamed. "That shit hurt! Untie me right now, you fucking bitch."

"Not 'til you tell me the truth."

"What truth?"

"That you were fuckin' Devin's wife," I said and cut him again.

"Ouch!" Winston screamed.

He jerked and pulled on his bonds, but he couldn't get loose. "Listen, white boy, I'm 'bout to cut this little mutha fucka off if don't start tellin' me the truth."

"If I tell you, will you untie me?"

"As long as you tell me the truth."

"All right then. Yes, I was fuckin' her. I would go over there at night when Devin left, and fuck her. Now you untie me right now."

"You were there the night she got killed, weren't you?"

"How do you know that?"

"Answer me!" I yelled, and made another motion toward his dick.

"Yes, okay, yes. I was there, but I didn't kill her."

"Devin said she takes sleeping pills and she would be asleep when he left the house at night. What was she doin'; fakin' him out with the pills?"

White boy looked away from me and didn't say anything. "Answer me!" I screamed, and cut him again.

"Okay!–She wasn't faking. She didn't even know I was there."

'What are you sayin'?" I asked with a frown on my face.

"I would fuck her after she passed out. But I didn't kill her."

"That shit is disgusting, white boy." All I could think about was my mama's drunk-ass man rapin' me. Taking advantage of her while she was defenseless, and couldn't do shit to stop his ass.

"Whatever; just untie me."

"I don't think so. Sick mutha fuckas like you don't deserve to breathe." I cut off his dick, and then I cut his throat. I got dressed, and once again, had to wipe down the room before I left. I took the stairs down and thought, *There's a lot of sick mutha fuckas in the world.*

Chapter Thirty-one

Avonte

After three hours of waiting, Detective Jensen finally told me that for the most part, my alibi checked out, and that I was free to go. "If you can think of anything that could be help, please give me call."

Before I left, Jensen promised that she would call me and let me know how things were proceeding with her investigation. That was three days ago, and I hadn't heard anything from her, so I decided to give her a call.

"This is Detective Jensen," she answered.

"Good afternoon, Detective Jensen. This is Avonte Petrocelli."

"Yes, Mrs. Petrocelli. What can I do for you?"

"Well, I hadn't heard from you, so I was just wondering if you had found my husband's killer."

"I'm sorry to say that we haven't made an arrest yet. But I assure you that we are doing everything we can. Mr. Petrocelli was last seen at bar called Shooters. Are you familiar with the place?"

"Yes, it's not far from the house."

"He was seen there on the night of the murder with two women. The woman he was found with, Laurie Springs, and an unidentified black woman. Witnesses describe her as being about five eight, dark complexion with long, straight black hair. Do you know if he knew anybody that matches that description?"

My breath got short. "Not that I know of. Do you think she killed him?"

"At this point, I'd just like to talk to her."

"I understand."

"I've gotta go, Mrs. Petrocelli, but I promise, I will let you know if anything changes."

"Thank you, detective," I said, and she hung up the phone.

My hands started shaking, because I knew from the description that the woman they were looking for was Qianna.

I hadn't spoken to her since that night she said she had something that she needed to take care of. Normally, I'd have been losing my mind about not hearing from her. But I've been so consumed with Tyrone's death, making arrangements for his funeral, and with being a suspect in his murder, that I haven't really had a chance to think about it.

I started to call her cell, but hung up the phone quickly. Suppose the cops had my phone tapped, and were just waiting for me to lead them to Qianna? If the police tie her to me, they are gonna think that Qianna killed Tyrone for me.

I tried to calm myself down because I knew I was trippin', and I had to think about what to do. I didn't know for sure if she really killed him or not, but I had to find out. I got up and got ready to leave the apartment.

But suppose they're outside waiting for me to lead them to her?

"Stop it, girl, you trippin'," I told myself, and grabbed my keys.

I never knew where Qianna lived, probably because she never told me. So I decided to look for her the only other place I knew her to be.

Just in case somebody was following me, I left the apartment walking quickly, like I was late for something. I got on the subway and took the train to the Times Square station. I got off the train, ran up the stairs, and tried to lose myself in the crowd. When I got outside, I hopped in a cab and gave the driver Angel's address. As we drove away, I sat in the backseat and felt foolish.

When we got to the building, I stood outside and looked around for a while, before I went inside. I was about to ring the bell when the door opened. Angel looked startled at first, but then she smiled when she saw me standing there. "Hello, Avonte."

"Hi, Angel."

"Come in," she said, and stepped aside. Qianna was right about one thing, Angel was a cutie. "Why don't you have a seat?"

"Thank you." Angel came and sat down next to me. "I don't mean to bother you."

"You're not bothering me," Angel said, and touched my hand. I looked at her eyes; those angel eyes. "I was just on my way out, so I was surprised to see you standing there; that's all."

"I know, and I'm sorry to just show up here like this, but I need to talk to Qianna. Have you seen her?"

"I thought you came to see me." Angel pulled her hand back slowly and looked away. "Qianna's in the back."

She looked disappointed that I was there to see Qianna and not her. I thought about how Qianna would talk about Cutie, and the things she could do with her strap.

"Angel," I said, and touched her hand.

She turned and looked at me.

"It's important that I talk to Qianna right now, and you're on your way out. Maybe we could get together another time."

Angel stood up and went in the back without saying anything. When she came back, she handed me a piece of paper and sat down next to me. "When you've had enough of Qianna, and her shit, call me."

"I'll do that," I promised, and quickly got something to write my cell number on, and handed it to her.

She looked at the number and smiled at me with those angel eyes. Angel kissed me on the cheek. "Like I said, Qianna's in the back. She'll be out in a minute," she said and left.

When I looked up, Qianna was standing in the doorway. She had cut her hair short and dyed it auburn. "It ain't like I'm not glad to see you, but, what you doin' here?"

"I needed to talk to you." I stood up and went to her.

Qianna held me by the back of my neck and kissed me. It makes me wet every time she does that.

"Yeah, but this is Cutie's spot. You can't just show up like this."

"I know that, and I apologized to Angel for just showing up like this, but I need to talk to you."

"You need to talk or you need something else?" Qianna asked, and smiled.

"No." I stepped away from her and sat down. I clasped my fingers together, and took a deep breath. "I really need to talk to you."

"What wrong now?" Qianna sat down next to me.

"Tyrone is dead."

"I'm sorry to hear that. Now he can't cutoff your money. Now you can have it all. You should be happy."

Truth be told, I hadn't really given *that* much thought either, but she was right. Unless he was lying to me, Weinstein didn't know why Tyrone cutoff the money, and to my knowledge, I was still in his will. I could come out of this on my feet, if I didn't go to jail. "The police questioned me about the murder."

"What did you tell them?"

"The truth. That I was home alone, on the phone talking to my parents."

"They buy that?"

"I told you, it was the truth."

"That don't mean nothin'. If the cops wanna pin something on you, ain't shit you can do to stop them."

"They said they were looking for an unidentified black woman about five eight, dark complexion with long, straight black hair," I said, and ran my hand through Qianna's hair.

"What else they say?"

"That he was last seen at a bar called Shooters. You know, the place I told you that he wanted me to meet him at that night. He was there with two women. The housekeeper found Tyrone and one of the women dead the next morning. They were both naked."

"They say anything else?"

"That's all the detective told me."

"Good."

I ran my fingers through her hair again. "Why'd you cut it?"

"I needed a new look."

"Why?"

"'Cause I needed a new look. Why you makin' a big deal of this? I cut my fuckin' hair. It's no big deal."

Sometimes she can be so frustrating to deal with. She knows what I'm asking her, but she is determined to make me ask it. "Are you the woman that the police are looking for, Qianna?"

"Wait here. I wanna show you something."

Qianna got up and went in the back. When she came back, Qianna was carrying a manila envelope, and handed it to me. "What's this?"

"Look and see."

I opened in the envelope, took out the contents, and began to read it. I knew right away that this was the information that Tyrone had gotten from the investigator he'd hired. "Where did you get this?" I asked, but I already knew. There was only one place that Qianna could have gotten it.

"Don't worry about that. The less you know, the better it is for you. So don't ask me shit you really don't want to know the answer to."

"You killed them?"

Qianna looked at me and shook her head. "What I just say. Don't ask me shit."

"But I'm asking anyway. Are you the woman the cops are looking for?"

"What you think, Avonte; that this shit just fell into my lap? Yes, I killed them."

"Oh my God." I dropped the papers on the coffee table, and buried my face in my hands.

"You should be thankin' me. Now you don't have to worry about that shit no more. You and me can go on livin' like we been livin'. Shit, now that bad-ass house he threw you out of is all ours."

"What if they find you, Qianna? They have a description of you."

"You said it yourself. They lookin' for some bitch with long black hair. That ain't me," Qianna said, and ran her fingers through her hair.

"What about fingerprints?"

"I wiped the joint down before I left."

Once again, my head dropped into my hands and I began to cry. I was crying because I was responsible for their deaths. Responsible as if I did it myself. I may have been mad at Tyrone, mad as hell, but I didn't want him dead.

"Look, Avonte," Qianna started, but I jerked away. "Oh, you don't want me to touch you now?"

"I'm sorry."

I heard her cell ringing in the other room. She looked at me like she wanted to kill me, and stood up. Without saying another word, she went in the back to answer it.

While she was gone, I thought about getting up and leaving. I could hear her talking; more like arguing with whoever it was she was on the phone with, and it sounded like she would be on it for a while. I started to stick my head in the door and say, *Hey, I gotta go*, but that would only make her madder. And that was the last thing I wanted to do.

Qianna had already killed Tyrone and some woman he was with. I didn't need her thinking that she had to worry about me rolling over on her.

So I sat there—like a good girl—and waited.

"Come here, Avonte," Qianna hollered from the other room. When I came into the room, Qianna was naked and laying across the bed. "Come here," she demanded, and I sat down on the bed next to her.

I didn't know what else to do, and was too scared to do anything other than what she told me to. I sat there watching as she stood, legs spread and bent at the knees.

When she stepped in front of me, squeezing her nipples and rubbing her clit, I inhaled her scent and felt my self getting wet.

"You want this pussy; don't even try to play like you don't." Qianna turned quickly and jiggled her ass in my face. "I see it in your eyes, Avonte."

I wanted to say, "Fuck you, Qianna. I never want you to touch me again," but I didn't say anything.

I couldn't.

As hard as I tried to speak, no words would come out of my mouth.

"Stand up."

Once again, I did what she asked of me. Qianna unbuttoned my blouse and unhooked my bra. She pressed her body against mine. In spite of everything, I was weak for her, and there was nothing I could do about it.

All I could do was shake my head. The sight of her large brown nipples took what little resistance I had. Qianna took one into her hand and squeezed it, as the other hand made a trail down to her clit.

"Take them pants off so I can taste you."

I took them off and lay down on my back. Qianna crawled above me on her hands and knees. She kissed me all over, and I wanted her to stop. But before I could protest, she kissed me hard and sucked my tongue. She tried to be rough, but Qianna's lips and tongue were so soft.

My clit was throbbing by the time she moved on to suck my neck. Then without using her hands, she took my nipple into her mouth and bit it harder than I liked, but even that shit felt good.

Qianna shoved my legs apart, and slid her body between my thighs. She attacked my clit and sucked it. I could feel it swelling.

Qianna was moving from my swollen clit to sucking my drenched lips. I used one hand to play with my nipples as the other held her head in place.

She used her fingers to pull my lips apart and sucked me from my clit to my ass. My juices ran down my cheeks, and she greedily sucked harder. Qianna shoved her fingers deeper into my warmth, and I could feel my walls contract and tighten around her fingers. No matter how scared I was of her now, Qianna still turned me the fuck on.

Chapter Thirty-two

Devin

"Hello, Devin, it's Avonte."

"Avonte," I said, more than surprised to hear her voice. It had been a couple of months since the last time we spoke, and she gave me the impression that it was over between us. "It's been a long time."

Avonte laughed a little, but it was a nervous laugh. "I know it's been a while since I talked to you, but you were on my mind, so I decided to give you a call. You know, see how you were doing."

"I've been all right, I guess. How've you been?"

"I'm okay."

There was a few seconds of silence, and then Avonte said, "I'm not bothering you, am I?"

"Not at all. What's up?" I asked, unsure of the reason for her call, and anxious to know what she wanted.

"Are you busy right now?"

"Not especially."

"I need to talk to somebody, so I was wondering if you could come by here."

"Where is here?"

"My apartment."

"I didn't know you had an apartment." The last time we got together, she was still with her husband. Avonte told me where she lived, and I told her that I would be there in an hour or so.

"I'll see you when you get here," Avonte said, and hung up the phone.

On the way over there, I thought about the tone of her voice. The tone of her voice told me that there was something she needed or wanted, and it wasn't just sex. Sex, I was down for, but I was in no mood for any drama. I had enough of my own.

It had been a week since the police came to the office investigating Winston's murder. As soon as I heard that he had been murdered, I knew Qianna was involved. I sat there petrified while they asked me questions, hoping that the truth wasn't written all over my face. "I understand that you and Mr. Hunter were friends, Mr. James," the detective began. "When was the last time you saw, Mr. Hunter?"

"He and I had drinks at a place not far from here called Bar 89."

"I'm not familiar with the place. Where is it?"

"It's on Mercer Street, between Spring and Broome."

"While you were there with him, did you see him talking to anybody there?"

"No," I answered quickly.

"How long were you there?"

"We had a couple of drinks, and I left him there. I can't believe he's dead," I threw in, partly because it was true. There was a part of me that didn't want to believe that Qianna had killed Winston. But when the detective told me that Winston's body was found tied to the bed with his throat cut, I knew that she had done it. "Can you tell me where you went after you left Mr. Hunter that night?"

"I came back here to catch up on some work."

"Did anybody see you?"

"Yes, I had to sign in with security when I got back to the building. And one of the cleaning crew saw me while I was here."

"What time was this?"

"I got back here about seven—seven-thirty, and I was here until some time after ten."

After the detective left the building, I waited a while before I left the building. I drove around for a while, before I stopped at a pay phone and called Qianna. "What did you do?"

"Who the fuck is this?"

"It's Devin."

"Oh, what's up, Devin? I didn't recognize the number."

"I'm calling from a pay phone. What did you do?"

"I don't know what you're talkin' 'bout. I do a lot of shit."

"Winston! What did you do to Winston?"

"You mean the freaky fuck that was fuckin' your wife?"

"What—what did you say?"

"I said the freaky fuck that was fuckin' your wife."

"Never mind that. What did you do?"

"You know what I did, Devin. I gave your boy what he deserved."

"You gonna get us both locked up."

"For what?"

"You know for what! The cops just left here. They know I was with him that night. Suppose somebody saw me talking to you?"

"What if they did? All they can say is that you talked to me and then you left. Nobody saw me leavin' there with him."

"I don't like this."

"So what if you don't. Look, nigga, you said it yourself; cops got a rape kit and his DNA, right? Once they match his DNA it's a done deal."

"And what happens then?"

"What you think gonna happen then? They'll think he killed her."

"And you don't think that they'll think that I killed him for it?"

"No. Cops aren't gonna think you had nothing to do with it. Not unless they think you had sex with him first. Listen, Devin, you don't know what that mutha fucka was doin'. He would wait until you left, and then he was fuckin' her after she passed out from them damn sleeping pills."

All of a sudden, something that Taye said to me once began to make sense. When Taye found out that I had sex with Sandra, she said that I forced myself on her.

"*Stop lying to me!*" I remembered Taye yelling that night. "I called your office—more than once; and never got an answer. Then you come home at ridiculous hours of the morning, do what you want to do to me, and run to the shower."

"What are you talkin' about?"

"You forced yourself on me!"

"What are you talking about?" I had never forced myself on her, so at the time I thought that Taye was really losing her mind. Now it all made sense.

Winston always did have a thing for Taye, but I would have never thought that he would have sex with her while she wasn't conscience. That shit was disgusting. No matter how disgusting I thought it was, I knew that once the police matched his DNA to the rape kit, I would be a suspect.

Yesterday, I got a call from the detective assigned to my case, asking if I would mind coming in to talk about the case. The detective told me that they were able to match the DNA sample to Winston.

"I don't know what to say. I mean, I would have never thought he would do something like that. Are you sure it was him?"

"We were able to confirm from some of your neighbors that they had seen his car parked outside your house on several occasions late at night, when you weren't there."

"And the robbery?"

"We think that it was just to cover up the murder."

It was lucky for me that I had an alibi for the night of his murder, or I would probably be in jail right now.

When I got to the address that Avonte had given me, I was a bit surprised at how nice a building it was. I went up to her apartment. "Hello, Devin," Avonte said when she opened the door.

"How're you doing, Avonte? You didn't sound too good on the phone."

"I don't know where to begin," Avonte said, and led me into the living room.

"Start at the beginning."

"It's about Qianna."

"I didn't know that you were still dealing with her."

Avonte looked away. "I kept seeing her after I stopped seeing you. She's like a drug to me. I can't seem to get enough of her."

Knowing how good the sex was, and remembering how Avonte used to get off on Qianna, I wasn't mad at her. A little jealous, but I wasn't mad about it.

"Why are you telling me this now, Avonte?"

"I'm afraid of her."

"Did she do something to you?"

"Not to me, she killed my husband."

"What?" I said, and thought, *Not you too.* "You had her kill your husband?"

Avonte looked like me like I had lost my mind. "No. I would never do anything like that. I had nothing to do with it. I told her that I had signed a prenup and he was cutting off my money," she said quickly.

"You need to slow down, Avonte," I said, and loosened my tie. "You need to tell me everything."

For the next hour, Avonte told me the truth about—about everything. How her husband told her that he was seeing another woman, and that's why she went to Puerto Rico.

Avonte said she came home to find the other woman in her house, and she moved out after that. She told me that the entire time we were together, she was separated and getting a healthily check every month. "Why didn't you tell me all this then?"

"I was confused and hurt after Tyrone did that to me. The things he said made me feel worthless. I wanted you to want me for me. Not because I had money."

"I understand you feeling that way, but I thought we had gotten past that, but I guess I was wrong. For a while I thought I was in love with you, Avonte. But I was just something for you to do; something to ease your pain."

"I'm sorry, Devin."

"You don't have to apologize."

She went on to explain that her husband had hired a private detective, and she showed me the pictures that he had taken of us together. "Where'd you get these?"

"Qianna got them the night she killed him."

"Are you a suspect?"

"No. I told you that I didn't have anything to do with any of that."

"So what's the problem?"

"I'm scared to death of her!" Avonte yelled, and started to cry.

"So what do you want me to do about it?"

"I'm sorry, Devin. I shouldn't have bothered you with this. It's my problem, and I'll have to work it out for myself."

Just then, I heard what sounded like a key hitting the lock. I looked at Avonte; her eyes were wide open in terror.

The door opened and Qianna walked in. She stopped in her tracks when she saw me. "What you doin' here?"

Chapter Thirty-three

Avonte

"Hello, Qianna," Devin said, and stood up. Just the sight of Qianna standing there had me scared. "I just came to say hello."

"I thought you said that he didn't know where you lived?" Qianna asked me.

"I–I asked him to come by. I needed somebody to talk to." I said. I wanted to run out of there, and put all this behind me. But once again, I was frozen by my fear; unable to move, and barely able to speak.

"Talk about what?" Qianna demanded to know.

"Nothing in particular," I said softly. "I just needed to talk to somebody, that's all."

"Why you shakin'?"

I wanted to say something. Tell her the truth–that I was afraid of her, and that I didn't want to see her anymore. But I couldn't.

Devin started moving toward the door. “Look, Avonte, I’m outta here. Call me if you need to talk some more.”

“No, Devin. Please don’t go.”

“That’s right, Devin. What’s you’re rush?” Qianna asked, and stepped in front of him. “Since you’re here, you might as well relax, have some fun. You know, like we used to. You remember how good we were together.”

“I got places to be. I don’t have time for this now,” Devin told her, and he tried to go around her.

“What you talkin’ ’bout? You always got time to get this pussy. You know how much you love gettin’ this pussy.” Qianna looked at me. “You want some of this dick, don’t you, Avonte?”

All I could do was nod my head. Sex was the last thing on my mind, but I definitely didn’t want him to leave. I didn’t want to be alone with her. After coming here and finding Devin, I didn’t know what she would do.

“Well I don’t. I told you, Qianna. I’m through with you,” Devin said.

“So you too good to get this pussy now; that what you sayin’?”

“Not too good, just not interested.”

“Well, get the fuck out then. You ain’t the only dick in town,” Qianna said angrily.

Once again, Devin started for the door. “Please, Devin, don’t go. Don’t leave me–”

“What’s goin’ on here?” Qianna looked at Devin, and then she turned to me. “You told him, didn’t you, bitch?”

I looked at her but didn’t answer.

“Answer me!” she screamed.

“Yes!” I screamed back. “I had to talk to somebody. I’m just so scared."

"What you scared of?" Qianna demanded. "I told you nothin' was gonna come of that shit."

"She's scared of you. I know you crazy, but you ain't that far gone that you can't see that she's scared of you." Devin said, and came to stand by me.

"So you told this nigga. This nigga? Bitch, please. This the last mutha fucka you needed to be talkin' to 'bout that shit. He ain't gonna care. Not after what he did."

"What are you talking about?" I needed to know. I looked at Devin. "What did you do?"

"Nothing, Avonte. It's not important now."

"Oh, you didn't tell her about your shit, did you, nigga?"

"Shut up, Qianna."

"Fuck you, nigga. I say what the fuck I wanna say, and ain't shit you can do to stop me."

"What did you do, Devin?" I asked again.

"Ask him about his wife, Avonte," Qianna urged.

"What about her?"

"Nothing, Avonte. It's nothing at all, nothing for you to be concerned with." Devin stepped toward Qianna. "You need to shut the fuck up."

"While you here spillin' your guts to this nigga 'bout me, he ain't tell you 'bout his shit."

"What happened to your wife, Devin?"

"She's dead!" Qianna said.

"I said shut up!"

"You killed your wife?"

"No!"

"No, the bitch nigga paid me to kill her."

"Oh my God." I started backing away from the two of them. Tears ran down my cheeks. He was just as bad as she was. The both of them were murderers.

Qianna grabbed me by the arm. "Where you goin'?"

"Let me go," I said, and jerked my arm away from her. "Both of you need to leave."

"I ain't goin' no damn where," Qianna said, and came toward me. I backed further away.

"Just get out!" I screamed. My head and my heart were pounding. I could barely see straight.

"Leave her alone."

Devin grabbed Qianna by the arm. "Get your mutha fuckin' hands off me, nigga."

"Get out! Both of you get out of here! I never wanna see either of you ever again!"

"Fuck that! Ungrateful bitch. Both of y'all ungrateful mutha fuckas. It ain't goin' down like this. Not today," Qianna said, and grabbed me with both hands.

"Let her go, Qianna," Devin said, and pulled her off of me.

Qianna broke free from Devin and swung at him. She reached in her purse and came out with a knife. She swung the knife at Devin, and cut him on his cheek.

Devin put his hand on his face and felt the blood. "You fuckin' bitch. I'll kill you!" he yelled, and started for her.

"Come on wit' it then!" As he came toward her, Qianna kept swinging that knife. She cut him on the arm, and again on his face, before he grabbed her. Devin reached back and punched her in the face. Qianna went down from the blow, but got right back up.

"Stop it!" I yelled.

"Shut up," Qianna said, and pushed me to the floor. With her attention on me, Devin was able to grab her.

I watched helplessly from the floor as the two of them wrestled for the knife. I knew I should get up and help him, but I couldn't.

Qianna got her hands free from Devin and she shoved the knife into his chest as he lunged for her. She pulled the knife out, and stuck it in his stomach.

Devin punched her in the face again, but then he fell to his knees.

I screamed.

Qianna backed away from him and watched as Devin's body shook a little, and he fell on the floor. She turned and looked at me. I saw the fury in her eyes and the blood dripping from her knife. I got up from the floor and ran in the bedroom. I closed the door, but she kicked it open before I could lock it.

"Now I gotta kill you too," Qianna said, and came toward me slowly.

"Please don't. Don't kill me. I'll do anything you say. I can give you money," I pleaded, and backed away from her.

Qianna pushed me down on the bed and crawled on top of me. She grabbed me by the throat and raised her knife.

Just as she was about to kill me, Devin wrapped his tie around her neck. He put his knee in her back and pulled both ends of his tie. Qianna struggled, trying desperately to get free, but Devin was too strong for her.

I laid there on the bed paralyzed by my fear, and watched as Qianna eyes opened wide, and she gasped for air. She dropped the knife, and then her body went limp. Devin let her go, and

Qianna fell on top of me. I pushed her off of me and jumped up from the bed.

I looked at Devin. "Are you all right?"

"Yes," I said, and then Devin fell on the bed next to her.

I screamed and shook him. "Devin, Devin. Oh, God, Devin. You can't die on me, not now." But he was dead. My whole body was shaking and tears were rolling down my cheeks. I backed out of the room slowly, and then ran out of the apartment.

Chapter Thirty-four

Avonte

When I left my apartment, I took the stairway down to the street and went out the back door. There were two dead people in my apartment, and unless she was kidding, and I don't think she was, one of them had killed three people. I still couldn't believe that Qianna had killed Tyrone, but to find out that she had killed Devin's wife for him was more than I could take in at one time. It took a while for me to calm down, and to think straight about what I was going to do next.

I knew at some point that the police would have to become involved. If that were the case, I knew that I would need a lawyer. I got myself together and walked to the first pay phone I could find, and was about to call Albert Weinstein, when my cell phone rang.

I pulled the phone from my pocket and looked at the display: Angel. I smiled when I saw her name. For a split second, I forgot that there were two dead bodies in my apartment, and I answered the phone. "Hello."

"Hello, Avonte. This is Angel. Did I catch you at a bad time?"

Instead of answering her, I started to cry.

"Avonte," Angel said. "Are you all right?"

"No," I cried even harder.

"Okay, just calm down and tell me what's wrong?"

I took a deep breath and tried to pull it together. "I can't tell you. Not over the phone."

"Okay, tell me where you are and I'll come to you."

"I'm at my apartment. Let me give you the address."

"No need. I know where you live. I dropped your scandalous friend off there before. I'll be there in about fifteen minutes," Angel promised.

When Angel got there, I was waiting for her outside, and we went in together. Once we got in the apartment, I finally told her what happened. I led Angel to the bedroom and pointed inside, because I knew that I couldn't go in.

Angel walked in the bedroom and looked at Devin and Qianna, dead on my king-size bed. "Devin?" Angel said quietly, when she recognized him.

"Do you know him?" I asked as Angel came out of the room.

"I met him at a club and we went out once," she said, and closed the door behind. Then she got a tissue out of her bag and wiped her fingerprints off the door. "Come on. Let's get out of here so we can talk."

We left the apartment and went down the street to the bar on the corner, and sat at a booth in the back. After the waitress brought our drinks, I told Angel the whole story. From the time I first met Devin in Puerto Rico, to our meeting Qianna, to what had happened that night. Once I explained it all to her, Angel looked at me. "Your shit is fucked up, girl." Angel pulled out her cell. "Let me see if I can help you get outta this."

Chapter Thirty-five

Angel

When Avonte told me her story, I knew that I had to do something to try and help her. She had nothing to do with all of those murders, but I knew just like she did, that if she called the cops, she would be hip-deep in their murderous mess. "Hey, girl. It's Angel, what's up?"

"Nothing much, Angel. What's going on with you?"

"A really dear friend of mine is in trouble, and she needs some advice on what to do," I said, and held Avonte's hand. "My girl here is a defense attorney."

I explained the situation to her and she listened quietly, and then she gave me her best advice.

"Okay, Angel, you said that the woman stabbed the man, and then he strangled her. Is that correct?"

"Yes, that's what happened."

"And right now, they are both in her bedroom dead on the

bed. Is that right?"

"Yes."

"Where is she now?"

"She's right here sitting next to me. We're at a bar down the street from the apartment."

"Good. Find out how long she's been gone from the apartment?"

"How long you been gone from the apartment?"

"No more than twenty-five, maybe thirty minutes," Avonte said, and I relayed what she said.

"Is there a store nearby where you are now? A deli or a liquor store maybe?"

"There's a liquor store about a block from here."

"Good, ask her if she has a credit card with her?"

"Avonte, do you have a credit card with you?"

"No, I just ran out of the apartment. I didn't bring anything with me."

"I heard her, and that's not good," Wanda said, and took a deep breath. "All right, tell her that what I need her to do is to go back to her apartment. Get a credit card and go buy something from that liquor store, whatever she drinks is fine. I need her to do this as quickly as possible, because the clock is ticking. Now, when she's been to the store and bought something, go back to the apartment. When you get in the room where the bodies are, I want you to scream as loud as you can. And then I want her to call the police."

"I understand."

"This is very important. What she's gonna to tell the police, is that the two of them came to her apartment together. That she left them there to go and get something to drink, and when she came back, that is how she found them. Do you think you can do that?"

"I don't know, Wanda. That seems like a lot of work."

"It's the best advice I can offer, Angel."

"That's okay, girl. Maybe I should just call Mike."

"If you think that's best, Angel. Give me a call and let me know if you or your friend needs me," Wanda said, and ended the call.

I explained to Avonte what Wanda said, and she wasn't feeling it either. "I got somebody else to call. In fact, I should have called him first." I dialed the number I had, and waited for somebody to answer.

"Hello."

"Hey, Victor, this is Angel, how are you?"

"Doin' fine, Angel. What about you?"

"You know me, always got something going on. Is he with you?"

"He's right here. Hold on."

"Who is it?" I heard him in the background.

"It's Angel."

"What's up, Angel?" Mike asked when he got on the phone.

"I need your help, Mike."

"That's the only time you call me these days, is when you need help."

"Well, you are my other big brother," I said, and gave Mike my innocent little-girl giggle. "Who else I'ma call but you? Besides, when my brother left the city, you said you'd look out for me."

"How is your brother, anyway?"

"I talked to Leon the other day. He said that things ain't all that good in da 'ville, and he might have to make a move back this way."

"Oh, yeah," Mike said, like he was glad to hear it. When Leon left New York it was over something Mike was involved in. Since then, Mike has looked out for me like a big brother. "You tell that nigga to holla at me."

"I will, next time I talk to him. But Mike, I'm for real, I really need your help."

"What's going on, Angel?"

"I don't want to go into detail on the phone," I said, and told him where we were. "I need you to come right away, Mike. Please don't keep me waitin' all night. You know how you do me."

"I don't know what you talkin' about, Angel," Mike said, and laughed.

"Yes, you do. I know you will hang up this phone and say '*she'll be all right*'. So if you ain't coming now, please tell me so I don't have to sit here all night lookin' like a fool."

"I'm coming right now, for real, Angel," Mike said, and I let him get off the phone.

I signaled for a waitress and ordered drinks. I figured that he would get there in an hour or two. So I was very surprised when I finished my drink, and looked up to see him coming through the door.

"Avonte, this is my big brother, Mike Black. Well–he ain't my real brother, but anyway. Mike, this is my friend Avonte."

"It's nice to meet you, Avonte."

I stood up. "Avonte, would you excuse us," I said, and took Mike by the hand and led him outside. I told him what Avonte told me.

"So what you call me for, Angel?"

"'Cause I like her, Mike. I don't want her to have to go through all that madness with the police."

"What you want me to do, Angel?"

"I don't know. I didn't wanna do all that stuff Wanda was talkin' about."

"You already talked to Wanda?"

"Yes."

"And what did Wanda want you to do?"

"Go back to the apartment and get her credit card, go buy something, then go back and call the cops. That was too complicated. Can't you just take care of this for me?" I pouted and folded my arms across my chest.

Then I gave him the look.

"Go get your friend, Angel."

"Thank you, Mike," I said, and kissed him on the cheek. I went inside and got Avonte, and the three of us went back to the apartment together. When we got there, Avonte showed him the bodies.

Chapter Thirty-six

Avonte

We walked as quickly as we could back to my apartment building. Once we got to the building, we went in through the service entrance, and returned to my apartment.

Mike—who was sexy as hell—told me to get whatever I was going to need from there. When we had my stuff together, Mike told us to leave and not come back, until he called Angel. I grabbed my purse and was about to leave, but I couldn't resist looking in the bedroom to make sure they were still there. I began shaking like it actually was the first time I had seen the bodies. Once I had satisfied myself that neither of them had come back from the dead, I left the apartment. I never knew what he did with the bodies, or how he got all the blood from the carpet or the mattress, but I couldn't tell that they had killed each other in there.

The problems began when the detectives asked me to come in, and began asking me questions about Qianna. It seems that in addition to me and Angel, Qianna had another lover. She reported her missing, and told the police that the last time she saw Qianna, she was on her way to my apartment.

Naturally, my fear was that they would figure out that Qianna had killed Tyrone, and they would assume that I was at worst, in on it, if I hadn't planned it myself. But the detectives only asked a few questions, which I answered honestly, almost. I told them that she never made it to my apartment that night. That I was out with a friend, and we had drinks at the bar on the corner.

A few days later, the detectives returned to my apartment and told me that Qianna was a convicted murderer, whose weapon of choice was a knife.

They told me that Qianna matched the general description of the woman that was seen with Tyrone at Shooters, on the night he was killed. At that point, I was sure that they would connect her to Tyrone's murder, and I would be arrested.

The investigation went on for over a week, and I ended up calling Angel's lawyer friend, Wanda. After Wanda spoke with the detectives, she told me not worry, that all they had was a vague description of a black woman, and that they couldn't place her at the scene of the crime. Wanda said that they'd shown her picture to some of the people who were at the bar that night, but none of them could positively identify her. I think that was the only thing that saved me, and I knew I had dodged a bullet.

When the case was finally laid to rest, I needed to get away for a while. Get out of the city and away from all the madness. But I didn't want to go alone. I could only think of one person to call.

"I've got to get out of the city for a while," I told her.

"After all you've been through; I can't say I blame you. I think that's a good idea. Where are you thinking about going?"

"I don't know, but I was thinking about just getting in the car, droppin' the top, and going wherever the road takes me."

"That sound like it might be fun. I wish I could just up and go like that."

"Well, to be honest with you, that's why I'm calling you."

"What do you mean?"

"I wanted to know if you wanted to come with me."

"Me?"

"Yes, you."

It took me a while to convince her, but I wore her down, and we planned to leave the next day. When I got to her apartment, she threw her bag in the trunk and got in the car.

"You ready to go, Angel?"

"As ready as I'll ever be," Angel told me, and we drove away.

End of

Killing Them Softly

Mike Black returns in Beneath The Surface